Dedications

To the fighters for Equality!

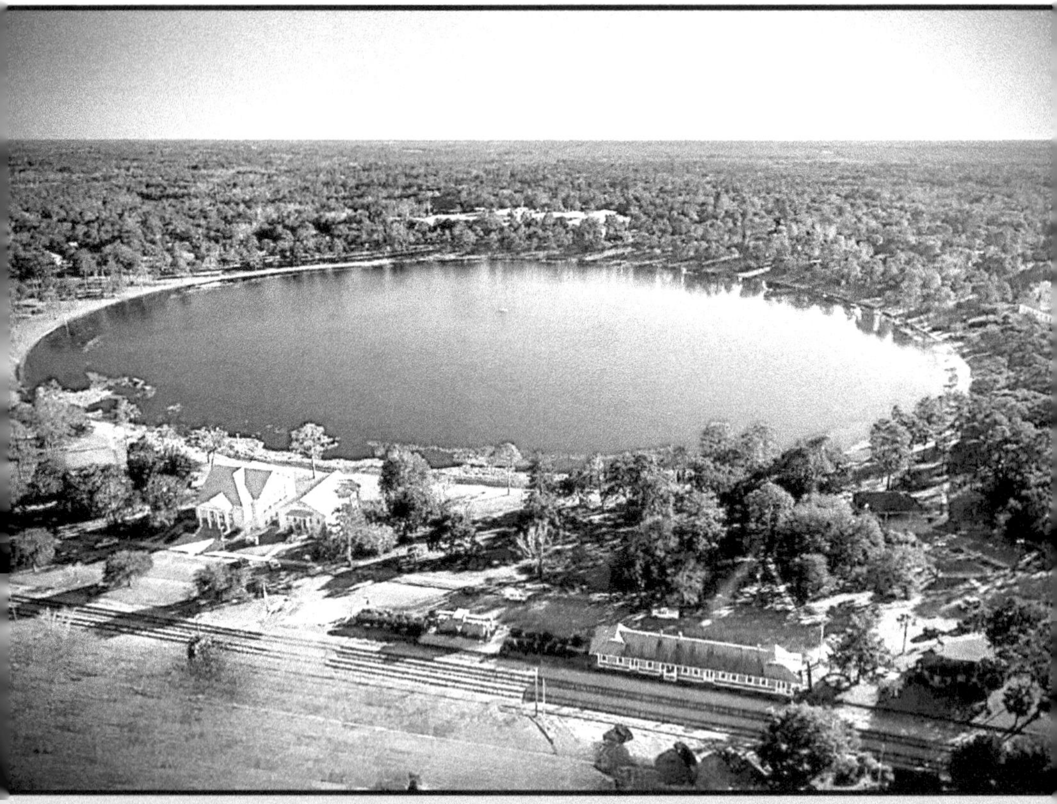

The Lake
Divided Waters

By
Tom McAuliffe

NEXT STOP PARADISE
PUBLISHING
Ft. Walton Beach, Florida, USA

The Lake
Divided Waters

by Tom McAuliffe

Copyright © 2025 - All rights reserved.

Any references to real people are coincidental. Real places are factual to the best of the authors memory, research and public records.

All rights to their respective holders. Usage credited. Educational-Historical documentation this non-profit publication is permitted by Fair Use copyright law.

FIRST EDITION - 2025

For more information email:
bookinfo@nextstopparadise.com

WWW.AUTHORTOMMCAULIFFE.COM

TABLE OF CONTENTS

Preface……………………………….11

Chapter 1 …………………………..17

Chapter 2 …………………………..39

Chapter 3 …………………………..65

Chapter 4 …………………………..79

Chapter 5 …………………………..91

Chapter 6 …………………………..105

Chapter 7 …………………………..121

Chapter 8 …………………………...131

Chapter 9 …………….……………..157

Chapter 10 …………………………..171

Extras:
Lynchings…………………….33
Desegregation………………..98
KKK………………………….185
DeFuniak Springs…………….190

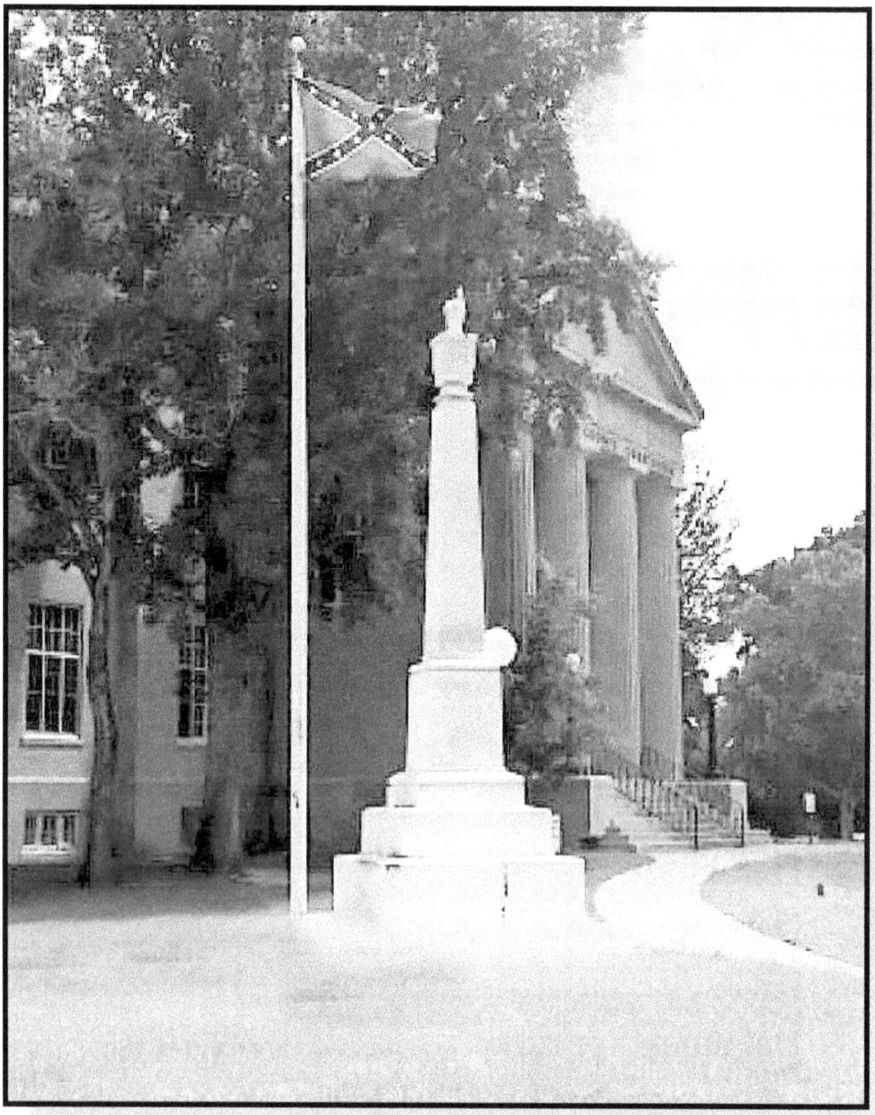

A NOTE FROM THE AUTHOR…

The N-Word
Dealing with a Legacy of Hate

Thank you for reading 'The Lake'. At the outset may we discuss something? It's not pleasant but… As you will see in the following pages I choice to use the word "nigger" throughout the narrative. It is a deliberate and painful decision, rooted in the desire to present an unflinching portrayal of the Jim Crow South. The language is harsh, raw, and real—a mirror of the times that refuses to soften the hard edges of history for the sake of comfort today. It's a choice that acknowledges the reality of the period, where the term was not just an common insult but a weapon—a linguistic embodiment of the systemic dehumanization that Black Americans endured under post civil war Jim Crow.

To understand the choice, the reader must enter Walton County in the early 20th century—a place like so many others in the South, where segregation was the law and white supremacy was in the air people breathed. The cotton fields, the segregated schools, the separate entrances to public buildings, and the rules about who could sit where on a bus—all of these were enforced by an unspoken, shared understanding among white and black (called 'Colored' back then) residents. They used "nigger" as more than just a racial slur. It was a term that defined and enforced power, a way of ensuring that the line between White and Black was clearly drawn and never crossed.

I tried to capture this linguistic reality to reveal the depths of a culture that considered Black people inherently inferior. To me avoiding the term would have been a betrayal of the truth. It was the word spoken in anger and in casual conversation alike, the marker of an entire society's internalized racism. In everyday exchanges between whites, "nigger" was a way to reduce a person to a category, to something less than human. It was a common word, but one that bore the full weight of oppression, signaling both an individual's supposed "place" in the social order and the ever-present threat of violence if that line was crossed.

Please know that the word's presence in the book is not there to shock for the sake of shock—it's a necessity for understanding. To ignore its usage would be to obscure the true nature of the power dynamics that structured the region's racial landscape. It was the word that punctuated the threats and punishments doled out in cotton fields, the word that was muttered under breath in stores when Black patrons dared to make eye contact with the White cashier, the word shouted from the porches of landowners to field hands, and the word used to justify and rationalize the terror of a lynching. It is a word that history cannot reclaim nor should it try; it is a reminder of the ugliest facets of the American past, the embodiment of racial terror given voice.

While it is semi-fictional, **The Lake-Divided Water** *aims not to offer an easy narrative of right and wrong but to provide a portrayal of a reality where a single word could mean everything. It was a word that signified a history of enslavement, of family separations, of Reconstruction's broken promises, and of the vicious backlash that followed. In the Jim Crow South, it became a shorthand for an entire culture of segregation, cruelty, and hierarchy—a culture that permeated every aspect of daily life in DeFuniak Springs, from the schools to the churches to the courthouse.*

By choosing to use "nigger" in the text, I'm sorry but I refuse to let myself or my readers hide from the discomfort of that reality. It's a choice that invites readers to witness history as it was, without the safety net of euphemism or today's sanitized language. It forces an acknowledgment of the deep and abiding scars that words can leave, and the ways those scars are passed down through generations. The language of the time—vulgar, cruel, and steeped in hate—was a weapon just as much as the rope or the rifle. To omit it would have been to do a disservice to the truth of those who suffered under its weight.

I believe the use of the term is, therefore, both an act of historical fidelity and a challenge to the reader: to confront what was said, how it was said, and why it was said, in order to understand the legacy of violence and inequality that has left its mark not only on Walton County but on the entire nation. It is a way of bearing witness, of refusing to allow the past to be whitewashed, and of demanding that the full story of the Jim Crow South be told in all its painful, unvarnished reality. To those offended please accept my sincere apologies and thank you.

PREFACE

This is a story about the power of community, the persistence of racism, and the slow but steady fight for justice. Through the lens of one small town in Northwest Florida it seeks to explore the larger struggle for civil rights in the south and America. Lake DeFuniak is a pristine natural *perfectly round* spring-fed lake one of only two in the world! With a circumference of 5,280 feet, about a mile around, it's an aquatic jewel loved by all in Walton County, the panhandle and the whole sunshine state. However its picturesque shores hide decades of past racial tension. Beneath the calm surface of Lake Defuniak lies a history of racial animosity and obstruction of social progress.

The Lake is both beautiful and symbolic and serves at the heart of our story. From the time Jesus rowed out from the shore with the disciples to modern day full emersion Christian baptism lakes have always had a profound meaning to most. And while unspoken or unpublished restrictions were a reality as far back as the 1920s although nothing was in a legal statute. Local blacks knew that there were only certain times they could 'get away with' a quick swim in the lake and certainly not when whites were swimming there. Back in the day it was not even contemplated. After all in 1920 one in 5 men in the South were members of the Klan.

Fast forward 40+ years and the administration of President Johnson in passing the civil rights act, voting rights act and similar legislation had basically made discrimination and race restrictions at public facilities like the lake, illegal. So rather than share the lake with 'the colored', town fathers restricted the lake so no one could swim there. This went on for more than 40 years. As the confederate battle flag flew over government buildings in the county and in the humid 100+ degree heat of the south no one could use the lake to cool off. No one. And this isn't ancient history… it's 1964!

In a special session meeting on May 6, 1964 — in the midst of strong southern opposition in Congress and locally to the proposed federal Civil Rights Act of 1964, signed into law by President Lyndon Johnson on July 2 of that year — the DeFuniak Springs City Council took action that shut down the lake ahead of the prospect of having Black and White people swimming together.

Nothing had changed since before WWII and the town elders in '64 made it very clear; nothing would change and that hell would freeze over before they'd see little Black boys and girls swimming with little White boys and girls. So like an immature 7 year old rather than share the lake's cool clear waters, they prohibited everyone from publicly using the lake. I say 'publicly' as it was common knowledge back in the day, that local law enforcement would allow the town elders and those of the fairer complexion who were well connected, to sometimes hold twilight swim parties on a hot Saturday night under torch light or in later years, the headlights of pickups lining the shore. It was the height of privilege and race restriction and it was one of the last vestiges of the old 'Jim Crow' south in NW Florida.

The term 'Jim Crow' typically refers to repressive laws and customs once used to restrict Black Americans' rights, but the origin of the name itself actually dates back to before the Civil War. In the early 1830s, the white actor Thomas Dartmouth "Daddy" Rice was propelled to stardom for performing minstrel routines as the fictional 'Jim Crow,' a caricature of a clumsy, dimwitted Black enslaved man. Rice claimed to have first created the character after witnessing an elderly Black man singing a tune called 'Jump Jim Crow Jump' in Louisville, Kentucky. He later appropriated the Jim Crow persona creating a minstrel act where he donned blackface and performed jokes and songs in an unflattering stereotypical dialect.

And even after 50+ years the confederate flag still flew above the county courthouse and city hall. It was only taken down in 2015. And even today we have monuments to the confederacy in our southern communities. Witness historic Seville Square in Pensacola which hosts a large obelisk memorial to confederate war dead. Like most I find these monuments an inappropriate salute to the treasonous who fought to destroy the United States of America. I feel it's also important to realize that the state of Miss. only ratified the 13th Amendment to free the slaves in 2013!

And to those who say it is all about "heritage and not hate'. I would submit it is both. The confederate battle flag is a flashpoint and is highly offensive. Many times when flown by locals it's about 'trying to piss off the liberals or the blacks' and done by young white men who have no idea who Andrew Jackson was let alone what the civil war was about. And to those that say it was about 'states rights'… you are correct. The right for those states to hold others humans as slaves because of the color of their skin. While it may be cute to dress up as confederate soldiers and officers thank god the men in Grey did not prevail.

Lake DeFuniak in DeFuniak Springs, Florida was closed in 1964 to avoid desegregation. The City Council closed the lake to all activities, including swimming, boating, skiing, and fishing, under the guise of water pollution. The decision was made after a petition from citizens, a report from the Walton County health department, and strong local opposition to the Civil Rights Act of 1964. After 57 years, Lake DeFuniak reopened for swimming in 2022. The lake is now open for swimming from March 1 through September 30 in a designated area behind the local library.

With effort and time now a place once stained by exclusion and injustice has become a beacon of hope for future generations both black and white. I live in the southland by choice and have for most of my adult life. While I may have been born a yankee and I still love my Detroit Tigers, I have the heart of a rebel. I love grits, moonshine, dirt track racing, Fishin, the FSU Seminoles, the

UF Gators and sunsets on the Gulf. It got in my blood since coming down in high school during the mid-70s. The south has come a long way since then and certainly from the old cross burning days of the Klan, although they're still around. Racism is much more subtle these days I hope this semi-fictional story pulled from historical documents and interviews, mixed with some fictional characters to help illustrate the story will illuminate the lessons of the old South.

I hope I've woven together an inspirational narrative showing that while progress may be slow and painful, it *is* possible. 'The Lake' helps its understand that the fight for equality is always worth the struggle. If the events of recent history have shown us anything it is that America and the southland have a long way to go to achieve true racial equality and harmony. Together I do hope we're on the road to a more perfect union.

Tom

2025

CHAPTER 1

The Good 'ol Days
Roots of Racism in Walton County

It is never too late to give up your prejudices.
Henry David Thoreau

DeFuniak Springs, nestled in the heart of Walton County, had once been a small community where nature seemed to defy the social and economic turmoil that plagued the rest of the South. The town boasted a lake with a perfect, circular shape, an almost miraculous marvel that was as rare as it was beautiful. Its waters had always been a place for gatherings—a haven of sorts where locals and visitors, black and white alike, could enjoy the cool escape from the scorching Florida sun. But that was before the Great Depression. That was before the racial lines, the ones that had always simmered beneath the surface of Southern life, hardened into immovable walls.

After reconstruction, like most of the southern states Florida passed 'Jim Crow' laws that segregated public facilities and transportation. This included restrictions on all public buildings and facilities as well as separate railroad cars and waiting rooms for different races. By the late 1930s, the depression's grip on the nation had been relentless, but in the South, where agricultural economies were already fragile, its effects were devastating. As cotton prices plummeted and tenant farming left both Black and White families destitute, the racial animosity that had always simmered began to flare into open hostility. Politicians eager to secure their hold on power amplified the message of segregation, offering white communities a false sense of superiority and security in the face of their own desperation.

In Walton County, as in much of Northwest Florida, this rising tide of racial hatred took on a cruelly pragmatic form. Jobs became scarce, and those that were available went first to the white workers. Schools, already inadequate, became even more starkly divided along racial lines, as did public facilities. And most symbolic of all was the transformation of DeFuniak Springs' beloved lake, once a shared retreat, now the focal point of segregationist policy. It became off-limits to the Black families who had enjoyed its shores for years. Quiet signs, first unofficial, later permanent, began to appear on the lakeshore: "Whites Only."

This was the world Elijah Johnson grew up in.

Elijah had always felt that the lake had a special pull, like a piece of himself lived within its waters. As a child, he remembered sitting by its edge with his father, watching the way the sun played over the surface, catching reflections of trees that stretched high into the sky. He had splashed and laughed there, the cool water licking his ankles while other children from town, Black and White, dove in deeper, unbothered by the world beyond the water's reach. Those were the moments that made life seem full of possibility.

But things changed. Slowly, but they did change.

It was the summer of 1933 when the first sign went up. Elijah was only eight years old, but he remembered it as clearly as the sunburned skies that stretched above them. He had gone with his father to the lake, eager to feel the cool water between his toes. Instead, he found himself standing beside a rough wooden post, staring up at the sign nailed to it, the words "Whites Only" glaring down at him.

His father, John Johnson, stood still for a moment, his expression unreadable. Elijah glanced up at him, waiting for a protest or for some explanation, but none came. Instead, John placed a gentle hand on his son's shoulder and said quietly, "We'll find another place."

They didn't, though. That was the reality. The other places didn't have the same quality of water, the same shade from the oak trees that Elijah had loved so much. His childhood had been cleaved in half by that day. It was a memory that marked him, a quiet ache that deepened over the years as he watched the lake become increasingly more of a symbol—a reflection of how Walton County drew its borders tighter around its white citizens while excluding the rest.

The Johnsons were no strangers to hardship, but John and his wife, Linda, instilled in their children a belief in the power of dignity and quiet resilience. Their small home in DeFuniak Springs was modest, the paint chipped and the roof in need of repair, but it was filled with warmth. Elijah's siblings, two brothers and a sister, helped their parents with the farm work, but Elijah had always been drawn more to books. Lila saved her pennies to buy him tattered copies of whatever she could find—history, poetry, stories from far-off places. She wanted her son to understand that there was a world beyond Walton County, beyond the rules of segregation that hemmed them in.

Elijah's quiet, determined spirit mirrored that of his father. John Johnson rarely raised his voice but commanded respect wherever he went. Even among white landowners who dealt with him grudgingly, there was an acknowledgment that John wasn't a man to be taken lightly. He knew his worth, even in a world that refused to recognize it.

As Elijah grew older, he carried that same quiet strength. He became acutely aware of the fact that his family lived under a constant shadow—not only of economic hardship but of the racial divide that seemed to tighten year after year. The lake was a particularly sharp reminder. Though he would sometimes walk by its edges, the cool water that had once been a source of joy now felt like an insult, a freedom denied.

In high school, Elijah watched as other Black families quietly left the county, seeking better lives in larger cities like Pensacola or farther north. But the Johnsons stayed, rooted in the land that had been theirs for generations. It wasn't out of stubbornness. John and Lila believed that running from Walton County wouldn't erase the broader struggle facing Black people across the South. The lines of segregation were drawn everywhere, but the Johnsons refused to let those lines dictate how they held their heads up.

In the late 1930s, as Elijah became a man, whispers of change were beginning to circulate. There were movements afoot, calls for Black communities to resist the injustices that had been so deeply woven into the fabric of Southern life. Though the violence of white supremacy was always a present threat, there was a growing sense that things couldn't remain as they were forever. Elijah was part of that hope, quietly watching, waiting, and learning.

He couldn't yet articulate it, but deep inside, he knew that he wouldn't live his whole life barred from the lake's waters. He might not have been able to sit on those shores in the way he once had, but he would find a way to protect the dignity of his family and his people. And maybe, just maybe, there would come a day when the signs that kept them out would come down, when the circles of segregation in Walton County would ripple out, like waves in the lake's water, until they were gone for good.

"De big bee suck de blossom...

De little bee make de honey...

De Black man makes de cotton and corn...

And de white man totes de money!"

- Song sung by Black field hands in the Jim Crow South

"There's a southern accent, where I come from, The young 'uns call it country, The Yankees call it dumb…
I got my own way of talkin', And everything is done, with a southern accent, Where I come from…"

Musician Tom Petty

For now, though, Elijah stood by the lake's edge, his hands shoved deep into his pockets, staring out at the smooth surface that stretched before him. The "Whites Only" sign was as familiar to him as the oak trees surrounding the water. It was a fixture now—one he'd learned to accept, though never truly forget. Even at eighteen, he still felt the sting of that first summer, the day the lake became forbidden. That summer had changed everything, marking the beginning of his understanding that the world was not as simple as it once seemed.

By the late 1930s, DeFuniak Springs, known simply as 'The Springs' by many locals, had become a microcosm of the larger forces shaping the South. The Great Depression had forced Walton County's economy to the brink, with failing farms and closed mills leaving both Black and white families struggling to survive. But as was often the case in the South, the brunt of the economic collapse fell hardest on Black families, who had fewer resources and even fewer opportunities to get ahead. Sharecropping, the primary occupation of many Black families, became an impossible cycle of debt and despair, as landowners squeezed every last penny from their tenants.

For white residents, the pressure of poverty only deepened their resolve to hold onto their racial privilege. Segregation became more than a way of life—it became a tool of survival, a desperate attempt to maintain some semblance of control in a world that seemed to be slipping away. Politicians in the South began to stoke the fires of racial division more openly, turning white fear into a weapon of political gain. In Walton County, where poverty was rampant, this meant enshrining racial segregation not just in schools or public services but in every corner of public life.

The lake, once a communal space for families of all races, had been an early battleground for these divisions. Before the depression, Elijah had seen Black and white children splash in its waters together. It hadn't been perfect, of course—racial tensions were always present in the South—but there had been a shared understanding that the lake was different, a place untouched by the rules that governed the rest of their lives. That had changed with the Depression, as fear turned into exclusion and exclusion into law.

For Elijah, the loss of the lake wasn't just about access to the water. It was about something deeper, something more personal. The lake had represented a fleeting glimpse of equality, a rare place where the color of his skin hadn't mattered. It was a sanctuary, and when it was taken away, it felt as though the possibility of real freedom had slipped away with it.

He turned away from the water and began the familiar walk back to his family's farm. The dirt path wound through the woods, past the occasional homestead, and into the clearing where the Johnson house sat, small but sturdy. His father, John, was working in the field, hoeing rows of corn under the sweltering October sun. Even in his late forties, John's broad shoulders and steady hands never showed the strain of the work, though Elijah knew his father felt it. It was in the lines etched deep into his face, the way his eyes seemed more tired with each passing year.

"Elijah," John called out, leaning on his hoe for a moment, "you walkin' by that lake again?"

Elijah nodded, wiping the sweat from his forehead. "Just thinking, is all."

John shook his head, his lips pressed into a thin line. "Ain't nothin' down there but trouble now. You know that."

"I know," Elijah said softly, but the ache in his chest told him that it wasn't that simple. The lake

STRANGE FRUIT

Southern trees bear
a strange fruit
Blood on the leaves
and blood at the root
Black bodies swingin' in
the Southern breeze
Strange fruit hangin'
from the poplar trees
Pastoral scene of the
gallant South
The bulgin' eyes
and the twisted mouth
Scent of magnolias
sweet and fresh
Then the sudden smell
of burnin' flesh
Here is a fruit for the
crows to pluck
For the rain to gather
For the wind to suck
For the sun to rot
For the tree to drop
a strange and bitter crop

Singer Billie Holiday, 1926

might have been forbidden to him, but its cool waters still called to him. It represented everything that was wrong with Walton County—everything he longed to change.

John paused for a moment, studying his son. "I know it don't seem right," he said after a while. "But we got to keep our heads down. The world ain't ready for what you're hoping for. Not yet."

Elijah looked at his father, his brow furrowed. He admired John's quiet strength, the way he carried the weight of their family with a dignity that no one could take from him. But Elijah wasn't sure he could live his whole life that way—waiting, hoping, but never fighting. "How long we supposed to wait?" Elijah asked, his voice betraying the frustration he felt. "How long we supposed to stay quiet, Pa?"

John sighed, resting the hoe on his shoulder. "As long as it takes. We keep our dignity by not lettin' them break us. By staying strong, no matter what they throw at us."

Elijah wanted to argue, but the words wouldn't come. He knew his father was right, in a way. The world they lived in was dangerous for Black families who didn't follow the unspoken rules of the South. Speaking out, pushing too hard, meant risking everything—livelihoods, safety, even their lives. But Elijah couldn't shake the feeling that something had to give. The signs, the separations, the constant reminders that he wasn't allowed the same rights as the white folks in town—it gnawed at him, day after day.

At night, after his family had gone to bed, Elijah would sit by the window, staring out at the moonlit fields. His thoughts often drifted to stories he had read about resistance, about people who had stood up against injustice and fought for something better. He had read about W.E.B. Du Bois and Marcus Garvey, men who spoke of Black pride and self-determination. Those ideas felt distant, almost too bold to imagine in a place like Walton County. But they stirred something in him, a quiet rebellion that he kept tucked away, hidden from the world, but growing stronger with each passing year.

He wasn't sure what his future held, but he knew that it wouldn't be like his father's. Elijah respected John more than anyone, but he couldn't see himself living out his days on the farm, content to keep his head down and wait for change that might never come. There was a fire in him, one that wouldn't be easily extinguished.

As the winds of World War II began to stir on the global stage, whispers of change were beginning to reach even small, isolated places like Walton County. Black men were being called to serve, to fight for a country that denied them basic rights. It was a cruel irony, but it was also an opportunity—a way to prove their worth, to demand respect in a way that words couldn't.

Elijah didn't know what the future would bring, but as he sat by his window, the lake and the sign barring him from its shores still burned in his mind. He couldn't help but believe that one day, things would be different. He might not live to see it, but he was determined to be part of the struggle, to carve out his own place in the world, no matter how long it took. He would not let Walton County break him, nor would he let the local system of the Springs define the future of his family.

LYNCHINGS - *A War of Attrition*

In DeFuniak Springs, the summer sun hung low in the sky, casting long, drawn-out shadows across the fields. The scent of freshly tilled earth mixed with the sweet, suffocating perfume of honeysuckle and heat, while cicadas droned lazily in the thick afternoon air. Fields of cotton stretched out like a white sea, the delicate bolls almost ready for harvest. For generations, these fields had been both a source of livelihood and sorrow. They were the thread that wove together the lives of the town's white landowners and the Black families who worked their land, though the stitching had always been raw and bloodied.

Joshua had worked the fields since he was strong enough to hold a cotton sack. He'd known no other life. As the eldest of his five siblings, he was up with the sun, picking row after row with the others while the overseer watched from horseback. It wasn't slavery anymore—at least not on paper—but the weight of debt and the endless need for survival kept Black families bound to the soil, locked in the cycle of sharecropping that had changed little since the Civil War.

They worked hard under the blistering sun, the brown of their skin turning darker with each season, backs bent and knuckles bleeding as the raw cotton was stripped from the sharp bracts. Once the picking was done, the cotton would be hauled to the gin, where the white landowners gathered to measure out their profits, sharing just enough with the families to keep them tied to another season's work.

The fields were never quiet, not really. As much as the Black folks kept their eyes down and minds on their work, they heard the whispers. And some nights, those whispers turned to threats carried on the wind—rumors of a new tension rising, of men riding out after dark, masked with kerchiefs and fueled by whiskey and hate. The word "nigger" fell from white lips like spit on the ground, an easy, ugly thing that kept distance between their world and the world of those who toiled in the fields.

Lynchings were an open secret, both feared and spoken about in hushed tones around kitchen tables. No one in the Black community dared to step out of line—fear was too heavy and its consequences too final. A flash of anger, a glance held a second too long, or simply a whisper of a rumor, and a life could be lost.

One evening, when the sky was purple and the air thick with the gathering dusk, a group of men rode down Main Street. The town went silent as their horses clopped in unison, the sound echoing off the shuttered storefronts and empty sidewalks. Joshua's cousin, Isaiah, had been accused of taking a sack of seed from a supply store—a claim built on nothing more than a white man's word and Isaiah's need to feed his family. There'd been no trial, no questions asked. The men had come straight to Isaiah's door, demanding he make himself known. They weren't there for answers; they were there for blood.

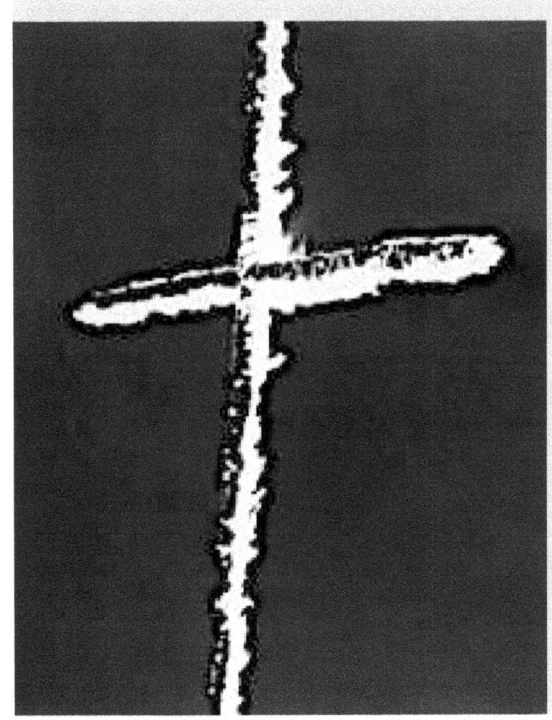

That night, the town

had the smell of smoke and gunpowder. The old oaks that lined the road bore witness to the horror that unfolded beneath their branches. The men who rode under the moon made sure their work was seen. In the dark, they became a shadowed mass of rope, torch, and rifles, slipping into the wooded outskirts where they tied Isaiah to a low-hanging branch.

By dawn, word spread like wildfire through the small town, carried by whispers in the cotton fields and among women doing laundry at the river's edge. Black families kept their children indoors and eyes low, whispering prayers that felt as though they would turn to ash before they left their lips. There would be no justice, no reckoning, only a quiet, unspoken mourning among the women in church who hummed low, sorrowful tunes when the hymns were over.

The white townsfolk called it a lesson, a reminder that their rules still held sway, even if the Union had declared otherwise. To them, the land had been blessed and cursed in equal measure—a place of prosperity for themselves, a reminder of subjugation for the rest. Cotton was their currency, and control of the Black population was the unspoken law that held everything together.
In the heat of that summer, cotton plants ripened under a blazing sun, their fields yielding both a crop and a history too heavy to bear. White landowners watched from their porches, cigars

smoldering and eyes sharp, ensuring that the color line remained unbroken.

The world turned slowly in DeFuniak Springs, caught between the glimmer of progress that the papers sometimes boasted and the iron grip of tradition that refused to die. What Isaiah's lynching had cost, the white community would never say out loud, but it remained in the eyes of every Black child who learned to keep their head down and hands busy—because life in DeFuniak Springs had a rhythm, and the danger was in disrupting it.

Each day began the same way it had for decades. The sun rose over the cotton fields, revealing rows that begged to be picked, while smoke from the night's terror hung invisible in the daylight. Mothers warned their sons and daughters not to question or challenge, while fathers went to work, silently praying for a season that would bring enough cotton to keep the debt collectors at bay. At church on Sunday, the preacher would speak of heaven's justice.

In neighboring Jackson County, nine African Americans were lynched after Reconstruction, including Claude Neal in 1934 and Cellos Harrison in 1943. Neal's lynching was covered by national newspapers and was followed by a white riot in Marianna. From the time of reconstruction after the civil war in the mid 1870's to 1965 when the civil rights bill was passed, the FBI estimates that there was at least one Lynching per week in the south… and this went on for 88 years! As time passed, the town closed its eyes and always returned to its routines. The cotton plants bloomed white, but for those who had watched the darkness of those times, there would be no forgetting. The fields that seemed so endless were small compared to the weight of memories everyone carried.

CHAPTER 2

Father Knows Best
The Town Elders

The perpetuation of slavery, the exile and extermination of American Indians, and the passage of Jim Crow laws were not carried out at the bidding of a few malefactors of great wealth.
P. J. O'Rourke

In this quiet town a small group of men held sway over every major decision. They were the town elders, a collective of older white men who had shaped the community's political, economic, and social fabric for decades. Each of them had come of age during the height of segregation and Jim Crow, and they believed fiercely in maintaining the traditions they had inherited from their fathers and grandfathers. Their power was rooted in both their wealth and their standing in the town, but more importantly, it was rooted in the unspoken agreement that the racial hierarchy they had grown up with was worth preserving at all costs.

For these men, the decision to close Lake DeFuniak rather than integrate it was not just about a single body of water. It was about defending a way of life they feared was slipping away—a world where they held control and Black people knew their place. The lake had become a symbol of their last stand against the tides of change, and in their eyes, it was better to close it entirely than allow Black residents the same privileges as whites. This moment would come to define not only DeFuniak Springs but also the broader history of Walton County and the South.

Mayor Walton Wallace was a reluctant leader but he strongly believed in the separation of the races. At the helm of the town elders the Mayor was a man who had inherited his father's hardware store and, with it, his father's reputation as a staunch defender of the old ways. Wallace had grown up in the Springs during the 1930s and 1940s, a time when segregation was not just law but an unquestioned way of life. His father, like many of the white men in town, had been deeply involved in local politics, ensuring that power stayed in the hands of those who understood the importance of maintaining the racial divide.

Wallace had never sought the limelight, but as the son of a prominent figure in the community, leadership was expected of him. When his father passed away in the early 1950s, Wallace took over both the hardware store and his father's position on the city council. By the late 1960s, when the issue of Lake DeFuniak's integration came to the fore, Wallace had become the town's mayor—largely by default. He wasn't a charismatic leader, but he was a steady one, and the town elders trusted him to keep things the way they had always been.

To Wallace, the lake was more than just a place for recreation. It was a symbol of white dominance, a public space that, like everything else in town, had been created for white residents. The thought of Black families swimming or picnicking alongside whites was anathema to him, as it was to the rest of the town elders and the locals at large. When the federal government began pushing for integration in the mid-60s, Wallace was adamant that it would never happen on his watch.

"There's no way we're letting that lake get overrun," Wallace had said during a heated town meeting. "I'd rather see it closed than turned into something we can't recognize anymore! Let the niggers go elsewhere."

And so, under his leadership, the town elders voted to close the lake rather than allow it to be integrated. It was a decision that would haunt the town for years, but to Wallace, it was the only option. He was convinced that allowing Black residents to use the lake would be the first step toward the total erosion of the racial order he had spent his life defending.

Now Billy Bob Richardson was the best Cotton Farmer in Northwest Florida with 7 farms and more than 5000 acres under plow. If Wallace represented the political power of DeFuniak Springs, Billy Bob Richardson represented its economic foundation. A local cotton farmer whose family had worked the same land for generations, Billy Bob was one of the wealthiest men in Walton County. His plantation stretched across hundreds of acres, worked by sharecroppers—most of them Black—who had little choice but to labor under the exploitative conditions Billy Bob's family had maintained since the days of slavery.

Billy had grown up during the Great Depression, a time when the South's economy was in shambles, and many white families feared they would lose everything. For people like Billy Bob's family, the only way to survive was to keep the racial hierarchy intact. Black labor was cheap and abundant, and keeping Black people in a subservient position ensured that white landowners like Billy Bob could continue to prosper.

By the 1950s, when Billy Bob was a young man, the cotton industry was in decline, but his wealth had been secured by generations of exploitation. He had little education beyond what was necessary to run the farm, but he had a deep-seated belief in the racial order that had benefited his family for so long. To Billy Bob, segregation wasn't just a law—it was the natural order of things.

When the town elders began discussing the possibility of integrating the Lake, Billy Bob was one of the loudest voices in opposition.

By strapping bags across their shoulders, enslaved workers could pick cotton with both hands. An average sack full of cotton weighed 75 to 100 pounds and each person was required to fill three to five sacks a day. This demanded strength and dexterity.

"I don't care what those people in Washington say," Billy Bob had growled at a town council meeting. "This is our town. Our land. We ain't gonna let them take it away from us. And we are not gonna let the Feds force us!" he said. "Ya know I treat my nigger workers good and they were happy before all this hubbub started!"

For Billy Bob, the lake wasn't just a place to relax on weekends—it was a line in the sand. If Black residents were allowed to use the lake, what would come next? Demands for equal pay for the sharecroppers? Black people sitting on the city council? The very thought filled him with rage. To Billy Bob, the fight over the lake was about much more than swimming rights—it was about maintaining the control that white landowners had wielded over Walton County for generations.

Then there's Charles 'Chuck' Thornton was the local mechanic, the kind of man who could fix anything with a motor. He was well-respected in the Springs for his practical skills. Unlike Wallace and Billy Bob, Bill wasn't born into wealth or political power. He grew up poor, the son of a dirt farmer who had barely scraped by during the Depression. But like many white men of his generation, Chuck had been taught that no matter how hard life was for White folks, it was always worse for Black people—and to his mind that's the way it should stay.

Chuck had served in World War II, fighting in Europe with the 101st Airborne and coming back with a deep sense of pride in his country and a drinking problem. The war had also exposed him to ideas that were foreign to the insular world of DeFuniak Springs. He had seen Black soldiers

fighting and dying alongside him. Black Men who had risked their lives for the same country he loved, but who came home to a nation that treated them as second-class citizens. At first, Bill didn't think much of it—segregation was just the way things were here and had been so since he could remember. But over time, the contradictions began to gnaw at him.

By the time the 1960s rolled around, Thornton was torn between his loyalty to his town and old school culture and the nagging sense that things weren't quite right. He had grown up believing that white people were supposed to be in charge and that Black people were inherently inferior. But he had also seen enough of the world to know that the rigid racial hierarchy of DeFuniak Springs was not as natural as he had once thought and that its days were numbered.

Still, when it came time to decide whether to integrate the lake, Chuck fell in line with the other town elders. He wasn't as vocal as Billy Bob or Wallace, but he cast his vote to keep the lake closed. Deep down, he knew that it was wrong, but he couldn't bring himself to go against the men he'd grown up with, men who had taught him everything he knew about how the world worked. Men whose sons and daughters went to school with his kids and whose wives were members of the 'Daughters of the Confederacy'.

"We've gotta stick together," Chuck had told his wife after the vote. "I don't like it, but it's just the way things are. We gotta make the niggers understand that!"

The legacy of the town elders is long and while the faces may have changed the efforts did not. The powers that be of the 1930's, 40's and 50's were of the same mindset as those who sit in influence there today. As the old saying goes; 'The more things change the more they stay the same!'

The town elders were more than just a group of powerful men—they were the embodiment of a system that had kept the South segregated for generations. They believed that by maintaining control over the lake, they could preserve the racial hierarchy that had defined their lives. But what they didn't realize was that the world was changing around them. The civil rights movement was gaining momentum, and even in small towns like The Springs, the pressure to desegregate was growing stronger by the day.

For men like Wallace, Billy Bob, and Chuck, the fight to keep the lake closed was about more than just a body of water. It was about defending a way of life that had been passed down to them, a way of life that was rooted in white supremacy. They couldn't see that their refusal to change was only hastening the end of the world they were trying so desperately to preserve.

As the battle over the lake continued, the town elders dug in their heels, refusing to budge. They held onto their power with an iron grip, determined to keep DeFuniak Springs as it had always been—

a town where white men called the shots and Black residents knew their place.

But the tides of history were turning. And though the town elders would continue to fight, their era was coming to an end. What they didn't realize was that in their stubborn refusal to integrate, they were sowing the seeds of their own defeat.

The decision to close Lake DeFuniak rather than integrate it would become a defining moment not just for the town, but for the entire region. It was a symbol of the South's struggle to come to terms with its racist past and the painful process of moving forward. For the town elders, it was the final stand of a generation that had grown up under Jim Crow, a generation that had built its identity on the notion of white superiority.

But for the younger generation—the students in Sarah Whitfield's classroom, the Black families who had fought for equality for so long—it was a moment of both deep frustration and awakening. While the town elders clung to the past, young people—both Black and white—began to question the legacy that had been handed down to them. The decision to close Lake DeFuniak rather than integrate it sparked a movement that would eventually dismantle the very system the elders had fought to preserve.

The social changes of the late 1950's and early 60s saw cracks in the foundation of the old south. By the mid 1960s, the fight over civil rights and over the lake had intensified. Protests became more frequent, with Black residents and their white allies demanding the right to access the lake. What had started as a local issue was now gaining state and national attention. Journalists from outside Walton County began to cover the story, and national civil rights organizations took notice. So did the Governor in Tallahassee. The town elders, once confident in their ability to maintain control, were beginning to feel the pressure.

Wallace , the mayor, found himself at the center of a storm he could no longer control. For years, he'd managed to keep the town in line with a mixture of old-fashioned authority and the support of his fellow elders. But as the protests grew larger and more vocal, even some of the town's white residents began to question the wisdom of keeping the lake closed.

"Maybe it's time to let it go, Wallace," Thornton said one evening as they sat in the back room of Wallace's hardware store, where the elders often met to discuss town matters. "People are getting restless. We can't keep this up forever."

Wallace shot him a hard look. "We've kept it up this long, Chuck. If we give in to the niggers now, what was the point of everything we've fought for in the past? Once we let them in the lake, ya know it won't stop there. They'll want seats on the council next. They'll want their kids in our schools. They will want to have their own businesses is that what you want?" he asked.

"How about a black hardware store!" Chuck joked. "Or a nigger auto shop?" Wallace shot back, clearly not amused.

Chuck fell silent, but the uncertainty in his eyes was clear. While he had voted to keep the lake closed, the doubts that had been festering in him since his time in the war were growing harder to ignore. He was starting to wonder whether Wallace and the other elders were not just fighting a losing battle but were wrong. It now seemed downright unAmerican to him.

Billy Bob Richardson is a reluctant realist who came to understand that chance is inevitable. Of all the elders, Billy Bob Richardson was perhaps the most pragmatic. A hard-nosed cotton farmer, he understood better than most how quickly things could change. The agricultural economy of the South had shifted dramatically in his lifetime, and Billy Bob had adapted to survive. But when it came to race, he had always held firm.

The rigid hierarchy that placed white landowners like him at the top of southern society had been a cornerstone of his identity, his livelihood and his community. He taught his kids that black people were OK they were just different. Still, Billy Bob was no fool. He could see the writing on the wall. The civil rights movement had already made significant gains in America and across the South. He understood that DeFuniak Springs wouldn't be able to resist integration forever. Yet, despite this awareness, Billy Bob felt trapped by his own history, by the expectations of his peers, and by the fear of what change might bring. At one of their private meetings, Billy Bob tried to voice his concerns.

"Wallace, you know I've stood by y'all through all this," he began, looking around at the other 'elders'. "But we've gotta face facts. This thing with the lake—the brouhaha is only getting bigger. They're not gonna stop. And if we don't find some way to compromise, we could lose a lot more than just the lake. We could lose control of the whole damn county and see our whole culture and way of life threatened."

Wallace stared at him in disbelief. "Compromise? You want us to roll over? After everything?!"

Billy Bob shook his head. "Nooooooo I'm not saying we roll over. I'm saying we think smart and long term. We're holding on to the Lake like it's the last stand, but if we don't adapt, we'll lose everything we've worked for. We've gotta be smarter than this. I say y'all give a little now to save a lot. Nothing less than the culture of our community is at stake here."

The room fell silent. Most of the other elders were getting uncomfortable with the direction the conversation was heading, but Billy Bob's words hung in the air. Even Mayor Wallace, for all his bluster, could see that the tide was beginning to turn. But he wasn't ready to give up—not yet.

Walton Wallace was known for his stubbornness. If there was one thing prided himself on, it was his unyielding nature. To him, compromise was a sign of weakness, and in his mind, weakness was what had allowed the federal government and yankee civil rights activists to encroach on towns like DeFuniak Springs in the first place. He saw himself as a defender of tradition and of a Southern way of life that he believed was under siege from outsiders.

"Ya know we've seen this all before... it's got nothing to do with racism and everything to do with outsiders coming down here and telling us how to live our lives. And I ain't havin none of it!" he said.

Back in the late 50's he once held up the town's first stop light for almost 3 years for fear it would spoil the small town feel of The Springs. And when it came to race relations? Wallace's conviction ran so deep that he was willing to sacrifice even the town's prosperity to keep things segregated. If not by law then by culture. But local business owners had begun to complain that the negative attention from all the protests and the media attention was hurting the little tourism they had and was driving potential customers away. The Mayor was unmoved.

"Guys we've been here before," Wallace told the elders at one of their meetings. Meetings that were purposely private to avoid the Florida civic meeting sunshine law mandating open and public meetings. "The outsiders come in, stir up trouble, and eventually they move on. This town will survive. It always has," said Wallace.

But what failed to see was that the world was changing in ways that The Springs could no longer ignore. The civil rights movement was not just a passing storm—it was a fundamental shift in American society. And as more towns across the South began to desegregate, the pressure on DeFuniak Springs and Walton County to follow suit only grew stronger both from within and without.

In every struggle there comes a critical mass for change. For Bill Thornton, the town mechanic, the fight over the lake marked a personal turning point. Unlike Wallace and Billy Bob, Bill had never been entirely comfortable with the role he played in upholding segregation. While he had gone along with the elders' decisions out of a sense of loyalty, the more he saw of the protests and the more he thought about the Black soldiers he had fought alongside during the war, the harder it became to justify his actions.

One night, after another long meeting where Wallace had once again refused to consider any kind of compromise, Bill found himself lying awake, thinking about his father. His father had been a good man, but he had also been a product of his time—a time when white supremacy was simply the way things were. Bill had always respected his father, but now he wondered whether respect meant continuing to uphold a system he knew was wrong.

The next morning, Bill did something he had never done before. He went to one of the community meetings organized by Lena Johnson and the activists who were pushing to reopen the lake. He didn't say much—just sat in the back and listened—but for the first time, he allowed himself to hear their side of the story without the filter of the town elders.

After the meeting, as he was leaving, Lena approached him.

"Bill Thornton, right?" she asked, offering her hand. "I'm Lena Johnson."

Bill shook her hand, feeling a mix of shame and relief. "Yeah, that's me. I just wanted to hear what y'all had to say."

Lena smiled, though there was a hint of suspicion in her eyes. "Well, I'm glad you came. It's about time some of you folks on the other side started listening."

Bill nodded, unsure of what to say. He wasn't ready to fully join Lena's cause, but something in him had shifted. He could no longer stand by silently while the town elders continued to fight a losing battle.

It was the end of an era… not with a bang but a whimper. In the years that followed, the town elders of DeFuniak Springs would find themselves increasingly isolated. Wallace remained as stubborn as ever, refusing to concede even as lawsuits mounted and public opinion began to turn against him. Billy Bob Richardson, though more pragmatic, continued to support Wallace out of a sense of loyalty and fear of what might come next. But Bill Thornton, after that fateful meeting with Lena Johnson, quietly withdrew from the fight.

The pressure on the town to desegregate continued to grow. Civil rights organizations filed lawsuits, and the federal government threatened to cut off funding to the town if it did not comply with desegregation laws. As the legal battles dragged on, the town's resources were stretched thin, and many white residents began to tire of the constant tension.

Finally, in the early 1970s, the courts ruled that Lake DeFuniak must be reopened and integrated. It was a bitter defeat for Wallace and the other elders, who had fought so hard to keep the town segregated. Wallace, who had staked his entire reputation on maintaining the racial order, resigned as mayor shortly after the ruling, his legacy forever tied to the lake's closure.

For the town elders, it was the end of an era. The world they had known—the world they had fought to preserve—was gone. And while DeFuniak

Springs would never fully escape the shadow of its past, the town began, slowly, to change.

As the town elders faded into the background, a new generation began to take its place. People like Lena Johnson and Sarah Whitfield—who had once been dismissed as troublemakers—became the leaders of a new DeFuniak Springs, one that was more inclusive, more open, and more willing to confront the painful legacy of its history.

Bill Thornton, though never a vocal activist, quietly supported these changes. He continued to work as a mechanic, but he was no longer involved in the decisions that shaped the town. He had seen enough to know that the fight for segregation was a losing one, and he was content to let the next generation build something better.

Billy Bob Richardson, meanwhile, focused on his farm, watching as the old ways of doing business gave way to new economic realities. He never fully embraced integration, but he came to accept that the world was changing… like it or not.

And Wallace? He remained a bitter figure, refusing to acknowledge that his defeat had been inevitable. For the rest of his life, he would rail against the changes that had come to DeFuniak Springs, clinging to the memories of a time when the town felt like it belonged solely to him and his peers. In the years following his resignation, he retreated further into his hardware store, becoming a relic of a bygone era—a reminder of the stubbornness that had once gripped the town.

With the lake reopened and integrated, DeFuniak Springs began to experience gradual changes. The once strictly divided community started to blend, albeit slowly and with resistance from some quarters. The lake, once a symbol of segregation and division, became a gathering place for families of all races. It was a small, yet significant step toward healing and understanding.

Lena Johnson emerged as a leader, her voice resonating not only in DeFuniak Springs but also in broader civil rights discussions across the region. With the support of Sarah Whitfield, she organized community events at the lake, inviting everyone—Black and white alike—to join in celebration, music, and dialogue. These events were not without their challenges; they were met with protests from those who still clung to the old ways, but Lena remained undeterred.

"Change is hard," she often reminded her followers. "But we have to keep pushing, keep standing together. Our children deserve to grow up in a world that doesn't define them by the color of their skin."

Sarah Whitfield, too, played a crucial role in fostering understanding. As a young teacher in the local school, she took it upon herself to educate her students about the complexities of their town's history. She shared the stories of the elders—not as figures to be glorified, but as cautionary tales of the consequences of ignorance and fear. Her classroom became a safe space for open discussions, a stark contrast to the silence that had previously suffocated such conversations in DeFuniak Springs.

"History is not just about the past; it's about shaping our future," Sarah would tell her students. "And if we ignore the mistakes we've made, we're bound to repeat them."

As Lena and Sarah worked to build a new community, Wallace and the Town Elders watched from the sidelines, increasingly isolated and resentful. He became a ghost in his own town, an ever-present figure that people acknowledged but no longer engaged with. His hardware store, once a bustling hub of community activity, now served as a backdrop to his bitterness.

While the younger generation embraced the changes, Wallace clung to his ideals. He often lamented the "good old days" when the town felt simpler and more predictable. His conversations with customers were tinged with nostalgia and anger, a longing for a past he felt slipping away.
"Things are different now," he would mutter, almost as if trying to convince himself. "People

don't understand what we've built here. The niggers are just tearing it all down."

But the more he complained, the more the community moved forward. New businesses opened, catering to a diverse clientele. Community events at the lake became a staple, showcasing local talent and celebrating the rich cultural tapestry of DeFuniak Springs. The lake transformed from a place of division into one of unity—a mirror reflecting the town's evolving identity.

Meanwhile, Billy Bob Richardson faced his own reckoning. The cotton industry was undergoing changes as well, with many farmers transitioning to more sustainable practices. He was forced to confront the legacy of his family's exploitation. As the younger generation became more vocal about workers' rights and fair treatment, Billy Bob found himself in a position he had never anticipated.

He began to hire workers from both Black and white communities, attempting to foster an environment of inclusivity on his farm. While it was met with some resistance from his peers, he recognized that to survive, he needed to adapt. He attended local community meetings, albeit reluctantly at first, and started to engage with leaders like Lena and Sarah.

"Listen, I might not agree with everything you're doing," he once said to Lena during a particularly tense community forum. "But I see where you're coming from. We can't keep doing things the way our fathers did. It's time to make some changes."

Lena regarded him carefully, appreciating his honesty but also aware that change wouldn't come overnight. "It's about time you realized that, Billy Bob. But this is just the beginning. We need real commitment if we're going to heal this town."

Slowly but surely, Billy Bob began to see the benefits of collaboration. He reached out to Lena and Sarah, and together they organized farm days that brought families together, fostering a sense of community beyond racial lines. While it wasn't easy, it was a start—a step toward a more equitable future.

Years passed, and DeFuniak Springs transformed before the eyes of its residents. The lake became a symbol of unity, a place where families of every color gathered for picnics, festivals, and celebrations of local culture. As summer faded into autumn, the townspeople began to embrace the change they had fought for so long.

The story of the lake's closure and the eventual fight for its reopening became part of the community's collective memory. It served as a lesson in resilience and the power of community action. Local schools incorporated this history into their curricula, teaching children about the civil rights movement, the significance of the lake, and the importance of standing up for justice.

Lena Johnson and Sarah Whitfield became icons of this new DeFuniak Springs. Their names were mentioned in discussions about community development, and they were often invited to speak at schools and events, sharing their stories of struggle, determination, and hope. Together, they demonstrated that real change was possible and that it could come from the grassroots.

As for Wallace, he faded further into the background, a reminder of what happens when fear and stubbornness cloud one's vision. Though he never accepted the new direction of the town, his legacy served as a stark contrast to the emerging future. The community learned that while the past could not be changed, it could be recognized, and that acknowledgment was vital for forgiveness.

By the end of the 1970s, DeFuniak Springs was no longer the insular, racially divided town it had been for generations. It was a place where diverse voices were heard, where the lake stood as a testament to the struggles of its residents—a symbol of what could be achieved when people came together for a common cause.

As Lena and Sarah looked out over the lake one sunny afternoon, they felt a sense of accomplishment. The air was filled with laughter, music, and the sound of splashing water as children of all races played together.

"We did it, didn't we?" Sarah said, her voice tinged with awe.

"Yeah, we sure did," Lena replied, her eyes shining with pride. "But this is just the beginning. There's still so much work to do."

CHAPTER 3

Wallace Remembers
Separate but Equal?

There's not an American in this country free until every one of us is free.
Jackie Robinson

Walton Wallace was a stalwart of segregation in the Springs and the county. He hade inherited the local hardware store and was the star quarterback in high school. It was also rumored that he was Klan. And everyone said he was also an asshole who thought he was better… not just better than black people… but everyone. Powerful as he was no one ever said anything to his face. Local racism was nothing if not polite.

Wallace was not just a mayor; he was the embodiment of a bygone era in Walton County—a time when racial segregation was not only a norm but an expectation in everyday life. Born in the early 1900s, Wallace grew up in DeFuniak Springs, a small town where race relations had long been defined by the harsh lines of segregation. His father had been a prominent businessman who owned the local hardware store, a tradition Wallace proudly continued into his adult years. The family had deep roots in the town, and with their status came a sense of responsibility to maintain the "old ways" that had governed DeFuniak Springs for generations.

As the owner of the hardware store and later, as the town's mayor, Wallace wielded significant influence in The Springs. He was one of the so-called "town elders," a group of prominent white men who saw themselves as the stewards of the town's history and traditions. For Wallace, that meant preserving the racial hierarchy that had existed for as long as he could remember. To him, segregation was not just a system of law and order; it was a way of life that had to be defended at all costs. He believed that any threat to segregation was a threat to the very fabric of Southern society. Nowhere was that belief more fiercely tested than in the battle over Lake DeFuniak.

Lake DeFuniak was more than just a body of water to the people of Walton County—it was the heart of the town, a picturesque, spring-fed lake that served as a gathering place for families, church groups, and social events. But by the mid-20th century, Lake DeFuniak had also become a symbol of the racial divide in the town. For years, Black residents had been barred from the lake, a policy that Wallace and the town elders defended with zeal. They viewed the lake as a "white space," a place where the community could maintain its racial purity, free from the presence of their Black neighbors. And that's the way it stayed for years!

1930s

1940s

1950s

Wallace had a deeply personal attachment to the lake. His father had told him stories about the days when the lake was first developed, when wealthy white northerners came to town for the Chautauqua gatherings and when the town's social hierarchy was firmly established. The lake, in his mind, was one of the last vestiges of that era—a place where the town's genteel, white community could escape the growing pressures for integration and social change that were sweeping across the South in the wake of the civil rights movement.

When Black activists, led by figures like Lena Johnson, began agitating for the desegregation of the lake in the 1960s, Wallace saw it as an existential threat. To him, reopening the lake to Black residents would not just be a concession—it would be a capitulation to the forces of "outside agitators" and "radicals" who sought to destroy the town's way of life. In Wallace's eyes, the lake had to be protected at all costs, even if that meant keeping it closed to everyone rather than allowing integration.

Defending the way things are was the order of the day. As mayor, Wallace used his position to maintain segregation in DeFuniak Springs, both at the lake and throughout the town. He had a natural charm, often hiding his more extreme views behind a veneer of Southern hospitality. To many white residents, Wallace was a man of principle—a steady hand who was dedicated to preserving the traditions of the town. But to the Black community, he was a symbol of oppression, a man whose policies kept them locked out of public spaces and opportunities for advancement.

Throughout his tenure as mayor, Wallace was a staunch defender of the status quo. He often invoked the language of "heritage" and "states' rights" to justify his stance on segregation, framing his opposition to integration as a defense of Southern values and local control. To Wallace, the federal government and civil rights activists represented an unwelcome intrusion into the affairs of DeFuniak Springs. He believed that the town should be able to decide its own destiny without interference from outsiders, especially when it came to matters of race.

Behind closed doors, Wallace was even more blunt about his views. In conversations with the town elders and local business leaders, he would often speak of the need to "keep things as they are" and prevent "troublemakers" from stirring up unrest in the community. To Wallace, any effort to desegregate the lake or other public spaces was a direct challenge to his authority and to the social order that he and his fellow town elders had worked so hard to maintain.

The battle over the Lake became the defining issue of Wallace's time as mayor. For years, Black residents had been advocating for access to the lake, organizing protests, and filing legal challenges to the town's segregationist policies. But Wallace was determined to hold the line. He used every tool at his disposal to prevent integration, from mobilizing the police to arrest protesters to enacting local ordinances that reinforced the town's segregationist policies.

When Lena Johnson and a group of Black activists organized a sit-in at the lake in the mid-1960s, Wallace was furious. He ordered the police to remove them by force, and several were arrested for trespassing. The sit-in drew national attention, and civil rights leaders from across the South began to take an interest in the fight for desegregation in DeFuniak Springs. But Wallace was unmoved. To him, the sit-in was a provocation, an attempt to undermine the authority of the town's leaders and force unwanted change on the community.

As the pressure mounted, Wallace became even more entrenched in his position. When it became clear that the courts might rule in favor of desegregation, he took drastic action: he proposed closing the lake entirely rather than allowing it to be integrated. To Wallace, this was the ultimate act of defiance—a way to send a message that he would rather see the lake unused and neglected than see it shared with Black residents.

The proposal to close the lake was controversial, even among some of Wallace's white supporters. Many white residents, especially younger generations, were beginning to question the wisdom of maintaining strict segregation in the face of changing social attitudes. But Wallace remained adamant. He viewed the lake as a last stand for the town's identity, and he refused to back down.

Despite Wallace 's efforts, the tides of change were sweeping across the South, and DeFuniak Springs was not immune to the forces of integration. By the late 1960s, the federal courts had ordered the desegregation of public spaces across the country, and Lake DeFuniak was no exception. Wallace fought the decision every step of the way, but in the end, he was forced to concede defeat.

The desegregation of the lake marked a turning point for the town. While Wallace continued to serve as mayor for several more years, his influence began to wane as younger, more progressive voices started to emerge in the community. The town's Black residents, led by activists like Lena Johnson, had won a significant victory, but the struggle for equality was far from over. Economic disparities, social exclusion, and racial tensions remained entrenched in DeFuniak Springs, and Wallace continued to represent the old guard—those who longed for the days when segregation was the law of the land.

In his later years, Wallace's hardware store remained a fixture in the town, though his once-ironclad grip on local politics had loosened. He continued to advocate for policies that reflected his segregationist views, but he found himself increasingly out of step with the changing social landscape. Many white residents who had once supported his leadership began to distance themselves from his extreme positions, recognizing that the town needed to move forward if it was to survive in the modern world.

For Wallace, however, there was no moving forward. He remained resolute in his belief that segregation had been a necessary and just system, and he never publicly recanted his views. Even as the town around him began to change, Wallace clung to the past, convinced that the integration of the lake had been a grave mistake that would have lasting consequences for DeFuniak Springs.

Wallace's legacy of racism is inextricably tied to the history of segregation across the southland over the years. He was a key figure in the town's resistance to integration, and his leadership during the battle over Lake DeFuniak made him a symbol of the old order—one that was built on the exclusion and oppression of Black residents. To many in the Black community, Wallace represented the worst of Walton County's racist past, a man who used his power to maintain a system of injustice and inequality.

But Wallace's legacy is also a reminder of the deep-rooted nature of segregation in the South. His views were not unique to him; they were reflective of a broader social system that had been in place for generations. Wallace saw himself as a defender of tradition, a custodian of the values that had shaped DeFuniak Springs for decades. In that sense, his life and career offer a window into the mindset of those who fought to preserve segregation, even as the world around them was changing.

Walton Wallace sat in his office, the weight of the town pressing down on him. The old wooden desk, scarred from decades of use, was littered with papers—petitions, complaints, and proposals he didn't bother to read. The town had changed, and every document in front of him was proof. Integration had swept across the South like an unstoppable wave, but here in DeFuniak Springs, Wallace had tried to hold the line.

To him, this wasn't just about politics; it was personal. His family had been in Walton County for generations, their name carved into the history of the place. They had built this town. But now, everywhere he looked, he saw things slipping away. The schools were integrated, businesses were hiring people "who didn't belong," and worst of all, he felt like the town wasn't his anymore.

"They're ruining everything," he muttered, leaning back in his chair.

The words felt familiar, like he'd said them a thousand times before. He stared out of the window at the town square below, where children of all races played in the park that used to be a place for white families to gather. The world outside his window wasn't the one he remembered, and the bitterness had grown like a poison in his gut.

It wasn't just the changes; it was the people behind them. To Walton, the rise of Black residents pushing for equal treatment, for a seat at the table, felt like an invasion. He'd never say it out loud, not in a public forum at least, but inside, the hatred festered. He'd heard the rumors about himself, the whispers behind closed doors—"Wallace is in the Klan." Some rumors were rooted in truth. He hadn't denied them, but he hadn't confirmed them either. There were some things best left unsaid.

He wasn't stupid. He knew that things had changed too much for him to speak the way his father or grandfather had. There was a time when people like him could say what they meant without fear of consequences, when segregation was law and people knew their place. Now, it was all different. The law wasn't on his side anymore.

But in Walton Wallace's heart, the hatred burned just as fiercely as ever.

He had grown up learning that the world worked a certain way, that it had to in order to function. Whites ran the town, owned the businesses, made the decisions. Everyone else lived on the margins, thankful for whatever scraps they were thrown. That was the way things had been, and that's the way they should stay, as far as Walton was concerned. Equality? Integration? Those were words he despised, because to him, they weren't about fairness—they were about destruction. Destruction of a way of life that had existed for generations.

He lit a cigarette, taking a long drag as his eyes narrowed on the distant figure of a Black man walking down Main Street. That man could vote now, sit in the same restaurants, and use the same public facilities, and it disgusted Walton to his core. He could still hear his father's voice in his ear, the lessons drilled into him about race, power, and how the South was supposed to stay.

"They've taken the schools, niggers taken the seats at the lunch counters, and now they want the town," he muttered bitterly. "But not while I'm still here."

There had been more protests lately. More people talking about equality, about fairness, about removing the Confederate symbols that still dotted the town. The old flag in front of the courthouse was a target now, the same flag Walton had fought tooth and nail to keep in place. To him, it wasn't about slavery or racism—it was about history, pride. It represented a South that didn't bend to outsiders. But no one seemed to understand that anymore. To him it was the principal of the thing.

The younger generation especially didn't seem to care about the values Walton held dear. Even the white kids were different, some of them marching alongside Black kids, calling for change. It disgusted him. "Traitors," he thought, sneering at the idea of white kids throwing away their birthright, turning their backs on their own people. He could hardly stand it.

A knock at the door pulled him from his thoughts. Walton stubbed out the cigarette, letting the embers die in the ashtray.

"Common in," he boomed.

It was Joe Thompson, one of his old friends, someone who had grown up with the same beliefs, the same ideas. Joe wasn't mayor, but he still had plenty of influence in town. And if the rumors about Walton were true, there were rumors about Joe too.

"Walton," Joe said, closing the door behind him, lowering his voice. "We've got a problem. People are talking about another march next week—this time, they're bringing in folks from Tallahassee. Big crowd."

Walton's face hardened. "What the hell do they want now? They've already taken enough."

Joe shifted uncomfortably. "They're saying it's time to take down the flag. For good. If we don't, they'll keep marching. The city council is already getting nervous."

Walton felt the rage rise in his chest. "That damn flag is staying right where it is," he growled. "I don't care how many niggers show up. This is my town, Joe. It's ours. We built it and we don't let them run us out. Ever!"

Joe nodded, but there was something uncertain in his eyes. Walton could see it, and it only made him angrier. The fear had spread. People like Joe, who should have been standing with him, were starting to buckle under the pressure.

"They've been pushing us for years," Walton continued, voice low and dangerous. "First it was schools, then the water fountains, then the goddamn lunch counters. Now they want to erase everything that stands for who we are. We give in now, we lose everything."

Joe glanced out the window, watching as a group of Black teenagers walked by, laughing, carefree. It wasn't the way things used to be. Walton could see that Joe was conflicted, but that only made him more determined.

"We've got to stand our ground," Walton pressed. "These niggers are not going to stop unless we make them stop."

Joe was quiet for a moment, his hand resting on the doorknob as if ready to leave. "Walton, times are changing. The council's already talking about compromise. I'm just saying… maybe we need to think about the future."

Walton's jaw clenched. "The future? You mean giving up?"

Joe didn't respond, and after a long silence, he opened the door and left without another word.

Walton stood in the quiet of his office, the shadows growing long as the day wore on. His mind was churning, hatred and defiance swirling in equal measure. He wasn't going to let the town he grew up in, the town his family had built, be taken from him by people who didn't belong. People who didn't deserve to be here. They might take his flag one day, but it would be over his dead body.

While Mayor Wallace may have been on the losing side of history, his influence on DeFuniak Springs cannot be denied. For better or worse, he helped shape the town's identity during a critical period in its history. The fight over Lake DeFuniak was not just about a body of water—it was about the future of the town and the legacy of segregation that had defined it. It was all about power and those who wanted to keep it at all costs.

80

CHAPTER 4

The 60s
A Time of Slow Change

Injustice anywhere is a threat to justice everywhere!
Martin Luther King, Jr.

Lena Johnson sat on her mother's porch, her fingers nervously twisting the edge of her Sunday dress. The Springs, as folks called it, was her home, and she had spent nearly thirty years watching its dirt roads stay the same. Watching the people she loved live small lives, fenced in by the invisible lines of race. But it was 1964, and something was shifting. Not fast, not with the speed the TV in the barbershop showed when Martin Luther King marched through the streets of Birmingham or when the President signed that civil rights bill up in Washington. But here, in Walton County, it was slower, like a rusting gate being pushed open.

The lake, was still segregated. No signs, no official decree, but everyone knew it. White folks swam and picnicked there while Black families gathered on the far side of the county for their outings. Even thinking about stepping foot in those waters invited trouble. Lena had heard the whispers, seen the sideways glances. The lake had become a line in the sand. To cross it meant daring to believe the world might change, but to believe that in Walton County could get you killed.

Jimmy Bedford didn't care much about getting killed. Not in the way most people did, anyhow. A white activist from Atlanta, Jimmy was reckless, always itching for confrontation, for the heat of battle. He had arrived in Walton County earlier that year, full of northern ideas and brimming with the fiery righteousness of a man who'd only known freedom. He was skinny, with sunburned skin and wire-rimmed glasses that made him look younger than his twenty-six years. To Lena, he looked like trouble. The kind of trouble that couldn't understand why change came so slowly in a place like this.

Lena Johnson stood at the edge of Silver Springs Lake, staring at the water. It was late, the dark stretching out over the surface like a thick veil, broken only by the faint moonlight. She could still hear the sounds of the day fading into the evening, the muffled laughter and splashes of white children, families enjoying the cool water on a summer afternoon. It had been like this for as long as she could remember—white folks at the lake, Black folks on the other side of the county, sitting by dusty ponds or not at all. Silver Springs was a symbol of what Walton County still held onto, even in the face of all that was happening in the country. The marches, the sit-ins, the Freedom Rides—it all seemed so far away here, where change was something to be feared and the old ways were clung to like a lifeline.

Born and raised in the Springs, Lena had lived her whole life watching her people pushed to the edges of public life, their presence tolerated only as long as they kept their heads down and stayed out of sight. But she wasn't one to stay silent. For the last few years, she had been organizing, quietly at first, then with more determination. Meetings in church basements, whispered plans for protests. The civil rights movement had come to Walton County, though it wasn't the tidal wave it had been in places like Birmingham or Selma. Here, it was a trickle—a slow, hesitant push against a deeply entrenched wall of segregation.

Lena knew the risks. She had seen the looks in the eyes of the white men in town, had heard the threats whispered just loud enough for her to catch. But fear had become a constant companion, something she had learned to live with, to push aside in the name of something bigger.

Then there was Jimmy Bedford, the white outsider who had blown into town with a fire in his belly and the air of someone looking for a fight. Lena hadn't quite known what to make of him at first. He was brash, reckless even, throwing himself into the movement with a fervor that scared some of the older folks, both Black and white. Jimmy had grown up in the North, far from the slow simmer of the South's racial tensions, but he had seen enough to know that Walton County was a place where things didn't change unless they were forced to. He came to the Springs looking for confrontation, looking to stir things up.

He didn't have to wait long.

The demonstrations had started small—a group of Black teenagers walking into the whites-only diner, Lena leading a handful of women into the courthouse to demand the right to vote. The reaction was swift. The town's sheriff, handpicked by Mayor Walton Wallace, made sure of that. Walton Wallace was the county's original segregationist, a man who had built his career on keeping things exactly the way they were. He was the gatekeeper of white supremacy in the Springs, and he wore that role like a badge of honor. He wasn't the kind of man to give fiery speeches like George Wallace or Bull Connor; he didn't need to. His presence alone was enough to remind everyone where the lines were drawn.

Under his watch, the county's Black residents were kept at the margins. They couldn't eat in the same restaurants, swim in the same lake, or sit at the same lunch counters. Wallace wasn't interested in compromise, and the growing movement in Walton County had only made him more determined to dig in his heels. Behind closed doors, he warned the business owners and the town's elders that any crack in their united front would bring the world crashing down.

Lena knew better. Change wasn't coming like a storm in Walton County; it was more like a slow, grinding erosion. And even as the national civil rights movement gained momentum, she could feel the tension building in the Springs. The undercurrent of rebellion was there, simmering just beneath the surface. The demonstrations were small, but they were courageous—Black and white activists, side by side, standing against a tide of threats and violence.

It was 1964, and the lake had become more than just a symbol of exclusion. It was a battleground. Jimmy Bedford had led one of the protests there, a small group of students from the local high school trying to wade into the water, only to be met with jeers from a crowd of white men, armed with baseball bats and bricks. The lake had closed soon after, boarded up and fenced off with a sign that read "Closed for Maintenance" that everyone knew was a lie. The truth was that Walton County would rather shut the lake down entirely than let Black folks swim in it. That summer, three civil rights workers were murdered just down the road, their bodies found buried in an earthen dam, and the lake's closure felt like a final, bitter retaliation.

Lena stood by the water's edge and thought of them—those young men who had come to the South to fight for freedom and paid the price. She thought of the lake, now silent and still, a monument to everything they were fighting against. She thought of Jimmy, who had gone back up North for a spell, but who had promised to return, determined to keep pushing, even if it meant more confrontation. And she thought of Walton Wallace, still sitting in his office, still fighting to keep things the way its always been.

But Lena knew change was coming. It was slow, painful, and dangerous, but it was coming. Maybe not today, maybe not tomorrow, but she could feel it in the air, like the first breath of a storm still far off but inevitable.

The lake might be closed, but the fight wasn't over. Not by a long shot.

Lena stood by the lake a moment longer, the weight of the summer heat pressing down on her, mingling with the suffocating sense of history around her. Silver Springs Lake, once a place of life and laughter for some, had become a symbol of exclusion for others. The men who jeered at Jimmy Bedford's protests weren't just defending a piece of property; they were defending an idea. The lake, in all its beauty, was a reminder that the boundary between white and Black, power and subjugation, wasn't just written into law; it was sewn into the fabric of daily life in Walton County.

But Lena had never been one to shrink from hard truths. She was born in these segregated streets, raised in the dusty shadow of white supremacy. Her father had been a sharecropper, one of the few Black men in the area to have a small plot of land to call his own, though never enough to escape poverty. He used to sit on their porch after long days in the fields, his hands cracked and calloused from years of labor, and tell Lena stories of when he was a boy, a time when the world was even more unforgiving.

"Things change slow, baby," he'd say, his voice low and worn, "but they change. You gotta keep pushing, even when you're tired."

Lena had taken those words to heart, and now, as the country seemed to be on fire with the flames of revolution and resistance, she couldn't just stand by. The church meetings, the quiet planning, the hushed conversations behind closed doors—they had all led to this moment, this fight. And it was a fight. Walton County might've seemed like a sleepy, backwater place to the rest of the world, but Lena knew better. Here, the battle for civil rights was not fought in grand speeches or televised marches. It was fought in everyday acts of defiance—in stepping where you weren't supposed to step, sitting where you weren't allowed to sit, swimming in waters that had been denied to you for generations.

But every act of resistance was met with force. Sometimes it was a subtle force—the mayor's office quietly pressuring businesses to keep their doors closed to Black customers, or the sheriff's deputies showing up just late enough to let white vigilantes send their message of hate. Other times, it was violence. Threats had become so routine that Lena no longer flinched when she found letters slipped under her door, telling her to leave town, or worse. The Ku Klux Klan didn't have to march through the streets in white robes for their presence to be felt. They were already there, sitting in city hall, running the police department, managing the local businesses.

And Walton Wallace, the mayor, was their figurehead. He didn't have to wear a hood; his suit and tie were enough. A tall man with thinning gray hair and a hard face, Wallace had built his reputation on maintaining order—the old order, the one where everyone knew their place. His office overlooked the town square, and he could see the courthouse steps from his window, where Black men and women dared to demand their right to vote. He could hear the rumblings of rebellion from the streets below. But as long as he sat in that chair, he would ensure that Walton County didn't change, not on his watch.

For Wallace, integration was a threat not just to his town, but to his very identity. He had grown up in the county, inheriting the family's small fortune from generations of cotton farming. The world he knew was one where the lines between Black and white were rigid, unbreakable. To him, the civil rights movement was an invasion—outsiders like Jimmy Bedford coming in, stirring up trouble, pushing people to question things that, in his mind, were not meant to be questioned.

Jimmy Bedford had become a thorn in Wallace's side. Unlike Lena, who had grown up in the Springs and had the cautious respect of the local Black community, Jimmy was an outsider, a firebrand. He wasn't afraid of confrontation—he seemed to thrive on it. When Jimmy had arrived in Walton County two years ago, fresh from the North, he carried the weight of his idealism like a badge. He had witnessed the sit-ins in Greensboro, had joined the Freedom Rides through Mississippi, and had stood in solidarity with Black activists across the South. But when he came to the Springs, he realized something different was required now.

The Springs was slower to change than other places. It wasn't the flashpoint of national attention like Birmingham or Jackson. It was smaller, quieter, its violence more subdued but just as insidious. Jimmy had learned quickly that here, confrontation meant something different. It meant risking your life every day, not just during marches or sit-ins. It meant living under a constant cloud of threat. He hadn't been prepared for the silence of the streets at night, for the way people would turn their heads when a Black person walked by, as if pretending they didn't exist.

Yet, he stayed. Something about the Springs called to him—maybe it was the stubbornness of people like Lena, who refused to give up even when hope seemed faint. Maybe it was the challenge of cracking the thick walls of segregation that still stood firm in this place. Whatever it was, Jimmy wasn't going anywhere.

The demonstrations had been small but powerful. Lena remembered the first one, a cold morning in February, when she, Jimmy, and a handful of local teenagers had marched from the Black Baptist church to the courthouse steps. They had stood in silence, holding signs that read We Want Freedom and End Segregation Now. No one spoke, but the message was clear. They were tired of being invisible, tired of being pushed to the margins.

It hadn't taken long for the sheriff to show up. Sheriff Hendricks, a burly man with a deep drawl and a reputation for keeping the peace through force, had approached them slowly, his hand resting on his gun belt.

"You folks know you can't stand here," he'd said, his voice flat and unmoved.

Lena had stepped forward, her chin held high. "We have a right to be here."

Sheriff Hendricks had smirked. "Nigger not in this town, ya don't!"

That day, they had been arrested. Not violently, but enough to send a message. In Walton County, even standing up for your rights could get you locked up. But that didn't stop them. The protests continued—small, steady, a few more people joining each time. But with each act of defiance, the threats grew. White men started gathering on street corners, watching them with narrowed eyes. Lena had found a brick through her window one night, a crude note attached that read, "Stay in your place."

The lake closing was the final blow of the summer. After the protest, when Jimmy and the local teenagers had waded into the water, it became clear that the white residents would rather lose access to their precious lake than share it. The county council, led by Mayor Wallace, had issued the order under the guise of "public safety," claiming that tensions were too high to allow the lake to remain open.

"They'd rather drown us all in it than let us swim in it," Jimmy had muttered bitterly the day after.

Now, Lena stood at its edge, wondering how much more they could take. The murders of the three civil rights workers—Schwerner, Chaney, and Goodman—had sent a shockwave through the community. They had been found just miles from here, buried deep in the Mississippi soil. It was a grim reminder of what could happen to anyone who dared challenge the status quo. But instead of cowering, it made Lena more determined.

"We're not giving up this fight," she whispered to herself, her eyes fixed on the still water. "Not now…not ever."

CHAPTER 5

Miss Johnson
A Voice of Defiance

Freedom is never given… it is won.
A. Philip Randolph

She was so Southern that she cried tears that came straight from the Mississippi, and she always smelled faintly of cottonwood and peaches.
Sarah Addison Allen

Lena Johnson was not someone who took "no" for an answer. Growing up in DeFuniak Springs in the 1950s and 60s, Lena was part of a generation that came of age in a changing South. Her father, Eli Johnson, had taught her the importance of resilience, of standing tall in the face of oppression, but also the limits of quiet dignity. Eli's generation, shaped by the harsh realities of segregation, had learned to navigate a world that offered little space for defiance. They kept their heads down and worked hard, hoping that things might slowly change. But Lena, filled with the fire of the civil rights movement, refused to accept the slow grind of change. Come hell or high water she was determined to create it.

Lena's fight to reopen the Lake—the symbolic and literal heart of the town—became the focal point of her life's work. The lake, which had been closed off to Black residents for decades, represented far more than just a body of water. It was a testament to the entrenched racial divide in Walton County, a reminder of the spaces where her people were told they didn't belong. But for Lena, it also represented hope. If she could win this battle—if she could restore access to the lake for everyone—perhaps it would signal the beginning of a deeper change in DeFuniak Springs.

Lena was born after WWII in 1948, in the twilight of the Jim Crow South. Her father, Eli Johnson, had grown up with painful memories of being barred from Lake DeFuniak as a child, and those stories became central to Lena's understanding of injustice. From a young age, she would sit by her father's side as he shared his memories of growing up in a segregated world, where the simplest joys —swimming in the lake on a hot summer day— were denied to Black children. Lena could see the sadness in her father's eyes when he spoke of the lake, but what struck her most was his acceptance of the status quo. Eli, like many Black men of his generation, had made peace with a world that told him he was less than. He had built his life around protecting his family and maintaining their dignity, never challenging the system directly.

But Lena was different. She had grown up watching the civil rights movement unfold across the South—Birmingham, Stone Mountain, Mississippi—and it stirred something in her. By the time she was a teenager, she had already made up her mind that she would not live in a world defined by segregation. Her father's stories about the lake only fueled her determination. She knew that the lake wasn't just about access to water; it was about power, about who had the right to claim public space and who was told to stay on the margins. For Lena, the fight to reopen Lake DeFuniak became a metaphor for the larger struggle for equality and justice.

The battle for the lake began quietly in the early 1960s, as the civil rights movement started to gain momentum across the country. Lena, then in her early twenties, was already emerging as a leader in the local Black community. Her fierce passion and refusal to back down made her a natural organizer, and she quickly became involved in efforts to desegregate public spaces in DeFuniak Springs. It started with lunch counters, where Lena and a group of young activists organized sit-ins, demanding service at the segregated diners downtown. They faced harassment, threats, and sometimes violence, but Lena remained undeterred.

The lake, however, was different. It was personal. Lena knew that reopening the lake to Black residents would be a symbolic victory, a declaration that they belonged in the town just as much as anyone else. But it was also a daunting challenge. The lake had been closed to Black residents for as long as anyone could remember, and the local government was resistant to change. White residents clung to the belief that the lake—and the town itself—was theirs, that maintaining racial separation was the natural order of things.

Lena began organizing protests at the lake, bringing together a coalition of activists, both Black and white, who shared her vision of a more just DeFuniak Springs. They held marches, rallies, and community meetings, drawing attention to the issue and demanding that the town's leaders take action. At first, the local government tried to ignore them, hoping the movement would fizzle out. But Lena was relentless. She knocked on doors, spoke at churches, and rallied the community with fiery speeches that stirred both hope and determination. Her voice was powerful, her words a call to action. "We will not be silent anymore," she would say. "This is our home, and we've every right to enjoy it, just like anyone."

Despite facing significant opposition, including threats of violence from local segregationists, Lena refused to back down. She was arrested several times during protests, but each time she returned to the front lines with even more resolve. "I wasn't afraid of jail," she later said. "What scared me was the thought of living in a world where my children would face the same barriers I did. That's what kept me going."

Lena's leadership extended beyond the fight for the lake. She became a central figure in the local civil rights movement, working to address issues like voter suppression, school desegregation, and economic inequality. Her home became a gathering place for activists, where strategies were planned and stories of resilience were shared. Lena had a way of bringing people together, of making them believe that change was possible even when the odds seemed insurmountable.

One of her greatest strengths was her ability to connect with people from all walks of life. While she was fierce in her activism, she also knew how to listen. Lena understood that the fight for justice wasn't just about grand gestures or headline-grabbing protests; it was about building relationships, about understanding the needs and fears of the community. She worked closely with local Black churches, knowing that faith was a central pillar of strength for many. She also reached out to white residents who were sympathetic to the cause, understanding that real change would require a broad coalition.

As the years went on, Lena's reputation grew. She was known not only for her activism but for her unwavering commitment to justice and equality. She took on local government officials, demanding accountability and transparency. She fought for better schools and more opportunities for Black families. And all the while, the lake remained her central focus.

In 1968, after years of tireless organizing, protesting, and legal battles, Lena and her supporters achieved a monumental victory. The town of DeFuniak Springs agreed to desegregate the lake, allowing all residents—regardless of race—to access its shores. It was a bittersweet moment for Lena. She had won the battle she had fought so hard for, but the journey had been long and difficult, and the scars of segregation still ran deep in the community.

For Lena, the reopening of the lake was a personal triumph, but it was also just one step in a larger fight for justice. "The lake is open, but the work isn't done," she told her supporters at a rally celebrating the victory. "We still have schools to desegregate, we still have poverty to fight, and we still have a system that treats us like second-class citizens. This is just the beginning."

Lena Johnson's legacy is one of perseverance, strength, and unwavering dedication to justice. She led with passion and conviction, never allowing fear or fatigue to slow her down. The victory at the lake was more than just a win for her; it was a victory for the entire Black community in The Springs, a symbol of their right to exist in the same public spaces as their white neighbors.

Lena's impact, however, went far beyond the lake. She inspired a generation of young activists, many of whom went on to lead their own movements for justice in the area and beyond. Her work laid the foundation for the ongoing fight for racial equality in Walton County, and her name became synonymous with courage and leadership.

In the years after the lake reopened, Lena continued to fight for civil rights, both locally and at the state level. She remained a voice of defiance, challenging injustice wherever she saw it. Her fiery spirit never dimmed, and even as she grew older, she remained a fixture in the community, mentoring young activists and reminding them of the importance of standing up for what is right.

Lena Johnson passed away in 2002, but her legacy lives on. The lake, once a symbol of exclusion, is now a gathering place for all residents of DeFuniak Springs, a testament to Lena's vision of a more inclusive and just community. Her life's work serves as a reminder that change is possible, even in the face of overwhelming odds, and that one person's determination can spark a movement that transforms a town.

Today, in DeFuniak Springs, Lena Johnson's name is remembered with reverence and respect. A park near the lake has been named in her honor, and her story is taught in local schools as part of the history of the civil rights movement in Walton County. For the people of the Springs, Lena Johnson is more than a figure from the past—she is a symbol of the power of perseverance, a beacon of hope for those who continue to fight for justice and equality in the South.

- The Coming of Desegregation -
The End of Separate by Equal

The courthouse in DeFuniak Springs loomed over the town square, its white pillars gleaming in the southern sun like the teeth of a clenched jaw. It had stood there since before the Great War, a monument to tradition, to stability, to the old ways that the white residents held so dear. Inside its cool, shaded halls, a different kind of battle was being waged, though few spoke of it openly. Rumors and resentment buzzed like gnats in the humid summer air, carried on the lips of men and women who had no intention of surrendering the world they had always known.

In the years since the Brown v. Board decision, the word "desegregation" had become a dirty word in DeFuniak Springs, spoken only in anger or in a low mutter, as if saying it out loud might make it real. The ruling had been met with outrage—first, by letters to the editor of the local paper, then by hushed meetings in living rooms and the back rooms of churches. White parents promised their children that they would not sit beside Black students in the same classrooms, while local politicians, bolstered by their constituents, made it clear that they would do whatever they could to delay and resist.

By the time the Voting Rights Act passed in 1965, the resistance had only grown more entrenched. The faces behind the desks in the courthouse were the same faces they had always been—descendants of the town's first settlers, families that had held power since long before anyone could remember. These men were determined that no piece of paper from Washington would change the way they ran their town. Outside, the century-old oak trees stood like sentinels, their branches heavy with the weight of history and unspoken threats.

At the Baptist church on Sunday mornings, the sermon was always the same, no matter the scripture: God's plan did not include the mixing of the races. Some preachers cited the story of Babel, others Genesis, finding whatever they could to justify their discomfort and their fear. The pews were full of solemn nods and amens as the congregation clung to the idea that the old order was the natural order—an order that ensured their schools, their town square, their neighborhoods would remain untouched by what they called "the chaos" that was spreading across the rest of the country.

Down at the soda fountain, men in starched shirts and straw hats gathered to sip coffee and grumble about the federal government, how it was sticking its nose where it didn't belong. They talked about "outside agitators" and how the marches on TV—those scenes of Black men and women demanding their rights in faraway cities—didn't represent the people in their town, the people who knew their place. "We don't need any do-gooders telling us how to live," they would say, puffing on cigars and wiping their brows with handkerchiefs.

When the summer of 1965 came and the news was filled with images of President Johnson signing the Voting Rights Act, the courthouse in DeFuniak Springs braced for what they feared—and quietly vowed to prevent. In secret meetings, local officials and civic leaders agreed on a strategy: delay, intimidate, and create every possible barrier

THE CHAUTAUQUA
HALL OF BROTHERHOOD

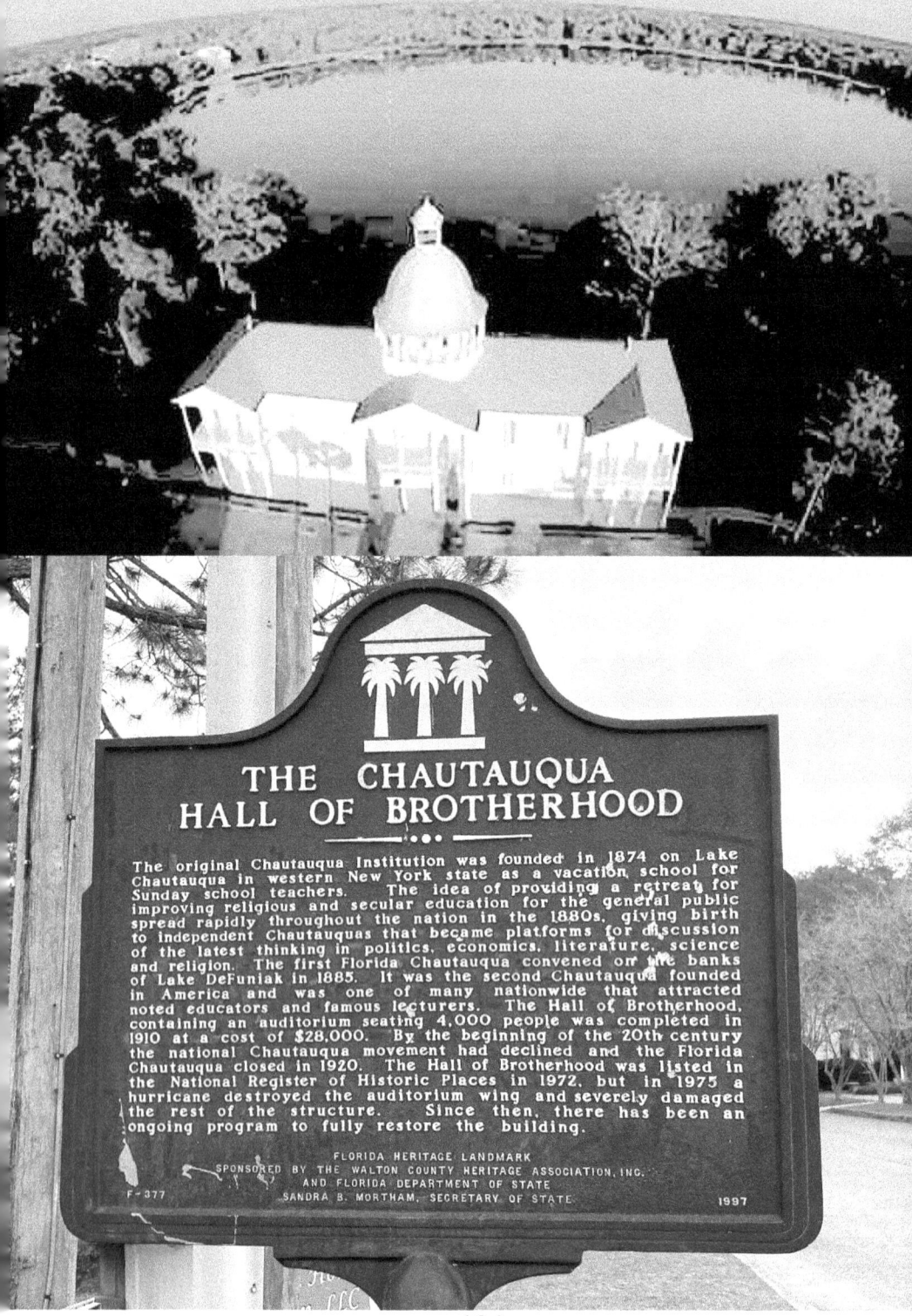

The original Chautauqua Institution was founded in 1874 on Lake Chautauqua in western New York state as a vacation school for Sunday school teachers. The idea of providing a retreat for improving religious and secular education for the general public spread rapidly throughout the nation in the 1880s, giving birth to independent Chautauquas that became platforms for discussion of the latest thinking in politics, economics, literature, science and religion. The first Florida Chautauqua convened on the banks of Lake DeFuniak in 1885. It was the second Chautauqua founded in America and was one of many nationwide that attracted noted educators and famous lecturers. The Hall of Brotherhood, containing an auditorium seating 4,000 people was completed in 1910 at a cost of $28,000. By the beginning of the 20th century the national Chautauqua movement had declined and the Florida Chautauqua closed in 1920. The Hall of Brotherhood was listed in the National Register of Historic Places in 1972, but in 1975 a hurricane destroyed the auditorium wing and severely damaged the rest of the structure. Since then, there has been an ongoing program to fully restore the building.

FLORIDA HERITAGE LANDMARK
SPONSORED BY THE WALTON COUNTY HERITAGE ASSOCIATION, INC.
AND FLORIDA DEPARTMENT OF STATE
SANDRA B. MORTHAM, SECRETARY OF STATE
F-377   1997

to keep things as they were. When the first Black men came to register to vote, they were met with cold stares and a list of impossible demands—a literacy test with questions that even the most educated white men could not answer, poll taxes meant to drain the wallets of those who could least afford it, and a "character reference" requirement that all but ensured failure.

"They don't want to vote, they just want to stir up trouble," folks would say, repeating it as if it were fact, as if saying it enough times would make it true. In quiet conversations, white men spoke of the "need to protect our way of life," their voices dropping low whenever they passed a Black man in the street. There were no direct threats, but everyone knew what lay beneath those polite refusals and the steel in their eyes.

In the years that followed, the town became a place of quiet defiance. The integration of schools was stalled with excuses about funding, facilities, and "readiness." When federal investigators came to see why so few Black residents were registered to vote, they were met with friendly smiles and vague promises that things would change—eventually. But behind those smiles was a wall of silence, a determination to protect the sanctity of the old South as long as they could.

At the barbershop, the old men still sat around the checkerboard, talking about how things were better "before"—before the marches, before the protests, before the government meddled in the affairs of good Southern folks. They spoke of "the troublemakers" who were stirring up unrest, their voices dripping with contempt. The barber's razor moved in slow, deliberate strokes, scraping away the stubble of men who saw the world slipping out of their control, no matter how hard they held on.

As the years passed, the resistance did not end, though it changed its face. Some of the more vocal white leaders in DeFuniak Springs softened their words in public, careful not to draw the attention of reporters or the federal government. But the anger lingered, simmering beneath the surface of polite smiles and handshakes. The signs that had once declared "Whites Only" were taken down, but their memory remained, etched into the minds of those who remembered what they called "the good old days."

It was said that DeFuniak Springs never really integrated—it just adapted. White parents found ways to avoid sending their children to newly integrated schools, moving them to private academies that sprang up almost overnight. The courthouse quietly complied with federal requirements but did so as slowly and reluctantly as possible, filling paperwork with loopholes and

creating red tape that ensnared any Black resident who tried to navigate it.

On Sundays, the town square still filled with the same faces, the same families, and the same unspoken understanding. DeFuniak Springs had changed, they said, but not in the way that Washington, D.C. had hoped. The sun still set over the white-pillared courthouse, casting long shadows over the land that had been theirs for so long. To them, they had not been defeated; they had simply held their ground—stubborn, unyielding, and proud of it.

FOR ALL DEPARTMENTS CALL
4500

Associated Press
Leased Wires

Late News

The Bee.

Danville, Va., Monday Afternoon, May 17, 1954

SEGREGATION IN PUBLIC SCHOOLS ENDED BY COURT

Ruled Unconstitutional By Supreme Court; Date To End Practice Not Set

Rules Separate Facilities Are Unequal

Danville School Board Will Meet At Once To Study Court Decision

Officials Give Views On Matter; Call For Calm Study On All Sides

Good Progress

Firm Entered, Haul Is Made; Boy Wounded

Man Accidentally Shot In The Hand

Paroled Slayer Captured After Bizarre Deaths

Held For Four Brutal Killings

McCarthy-Army Hearings' Future Thrown In Doubt

Presidential Order Shutting Off Inquiry Denounced By Sen. McCarthy

Suit Being Tried

Funds Requested

Considering Violations

CHAPTER 6

Sarah Whitfield
A New Voice

Hate is not natural… it is learned.
Mr. Rogers

Sarah Whitfield stood out in DeFuniak Springs. Born in the late 1940s, she came of age during the 1960s, a time of great upheaval across the nation. But even in this small town, the tides of change were beginning to stir. While many in the town clung fiercely to the values of the past, Sarah was part of a new generation of Southerners who questioned the racist norms they had inherited from their parents and grandparents. And it was in this small, conservative town—where the town elders maintained a firm grip on local power—that Sarah decided to become one of Lena Johnson's few white allies in the fight to reopen the Lake.

As a young teacher at the local high school, Sarah had a passion for history, but not the kind of history that glossed over the darker aspects of the South's past. She believed that the story of the South could not be told without addressing the full weight of its legacy—slavery, Jim Crow, segregation, and the enduring inequality that persisted even after the civil rights movement. For Sarah, it was not enough to teach her students about the Confederacy or the glories of Southern heritage without also teaching them about the horrors of lynching, the terror of white supremacy, and the bravery of those fighting for justice.

Her progressive views put her at odds with many in DeFuniak Springs, especially the town elders. Men like Wallace , the mayor, who had grown up with a deep reverence for the past and viewed any criticism of Southern traditions as an attack on their way of life. Sarah knew she wasn't popular with people like Wallace. She'd heard the whispers, the murmurs in the church pews, and the thinly veiled comments at the grocery store about how she was "teaching the wrong kind of history." But Sarah had never been the kind of person to back down from what she believed was right.

In Sarah's classroom, the walls were lined with books, maps, and posters—symbols of a world far broader than the insular community of DeFuniak Springs. She taught her students about Abraham Lincoln and Jefferson Davis, but she also introduced them to the writings of Frederick Douglass, W.E.B. Du Bois, and Harriet Tubman. She didn't shy away from uncomfortable topics. While other teachers in the town would skim over the Civil Rights Movement or portray it as a distant, resolved issue, Sarah made it clear to her students that the struggle for equality was ongoing, that the racism of the past had not simply vanished with the signing of the Civil Rights Act.

One day, during a lesson on Reconstruction, Sarah posed a question to her students that had likely never been asked in a DeFuniak Springs classroom: "What do you think life was like for Black families after the Civil War? After they were freed, but still surrounded by people who wanted to keep them in chains?"

The room went silent. Her students—mostly white, but a few Black—shifted uncomfortably in their seats. Sarah waited, letting the silence stretch. It was an important question, and she wanted them to think deeply about it. Finally, one of her more outspoken students, a boy named Matthew, raised his hand.

"I guess it must have been pretty hard," he said hesitantly. "Like, they were free, but they probably couldn't go wherever they wanted."

Sarah nodded. "Exactly. They were free, but they weren't truly equal, were they? In many ways, they were still living under a system that kept them oppressed."

She went on to explain the rise of Jim Crow laws, the terror of the Ku Klux Klan, and the violent backlash that met Black Americans at every turn as they sought to claim their rights as citizens. Some of her students looked shocked, as if they had never considered the brutal reality of life for Black people in the post-slavery South. For others, it was uncomfortable, as though Sarah was challenging the very narrative they had been raised to believe—that the South's history was one of noble struggle and that the Confederacy had fought for a just cause.

Sarah knew she was walking a fine line. In DeFuniak Springs, people were proud of their Southern heritage, and for many, that pride was closely tied to a sanitized version of history—one that glorified the Confederacy and minimized the brutality of slavery and segregation. But Sarah was committed to giving her students a fuller picture. She wanted them to understand that history was not just a story of triumphs, but also of deep injustices.

Sarah had first met Lena Johnson at a community meeting about the future of the lake. It was a tense gathering, filled with heated arguments over whether Lake DeFuniak should remain closed or be reopened to everyone, regardless of race. Wallace and the town elders had been clear—they would rather see the lake remain closed than share it with Black residents. But Lena was equally determined. She spoke with a fiery conviction that captivated Sarah, and though the two women came from different worlds, Sarah was deeply inspired by Lena's courage.

After the meeting, Sarah approached Lena.

"You spoke beautifully tonight," Sarah said, her voice full of admiration. "I want you to know that there are some of us, even in the white community, who stand with you."

Lena, who had long grown accustomed to white resistance, looked at Sarah with a mixture of skepticism and curiosity. "I appreciate that," she replied cautiously, "but we need more than words. We need people willing to take action."

From that day forward, Sarah and Lena began working together, forging an unlikely alliance in a town where such relationships were still considered taboo. Sarah knew that aligning herself with Lena and the fight for desegregation would only deepen the divide between her and many in the white community, but she didn't care. She was driven by a sense of justice, and she could no longer remain silent in the face of the discrimination and exclusion that had plagued DeFuniak Springs for too long.

Sarah represented a new generation of Southerners —young people who rejected the racist norms of the past and were determined to build a more inclusive future. While Wallace and the town elders clung to the old ways, people like Sarah were beginning to question the myths that had been passed down to them. She understood that being a Southerner didn't have to mean holding on to the legacy of white supremacy. Instead, she believed that the South could move forward by confronting its history honestly and working toward reconciliation and justice.

In her classroom, Sarah talked openly about the ongoing fight for equality. She encouraged her students to think critically about the world around them, to question the structures of power that maintained inequality, and to consider their own roles in shaping the future of their community. For Sarah, education was not just about imparting knowledge; it was about empowering her students to become agents of change.

At times, her progressive views put her at odds with the school administration. She was warned more than once to "tone it down" and to avoid controversial topics that might upset the parents. But Sarah refused to back down. She believed that her students deserved the truth, and she wasn't going to let local pressures keep her from teaching.

As Sarah became more involved in the fight to reopen the lake, the backlash from the town elders intensified. Wallace and his allies viewed her as a troublemaker, someone who was undermining the traditional values of the town. She was labeled a "radical" and accused of bringing outside ideas into the community—ideas that many believed had no place in DeFuniak Springs. Some parents even pulled their children from her classes, refusing to let them be "indoctrinated" by Sarah's teachings.

But Sarah stood firm. She knew that change was never easy, and that those who challenged the status quo were often met with hostility. Still, the attacks weighed on her. She had grown up in DeFuniak Springs, and in many ways, it was still home. But she could no longer ignore the deep racial divisions that ran through the town, nor could she remain silent in the face of injustice.

At night, Sarah would sit by her window, staring out at the quiet roads of the Springs, wondering what the future held for the town she had always loved. She knew that the fight for desegregation was just one battle in a much larger struggle for equality, but she also knew that it was a crucial one. The lake had become a symbol of the town's refusal to move forward, and Sarah was determined to be on the right side of history.

She was a woman of quiet determination. Sarah Whitfield's journey was not one of grand gestures or public accolades. Unlike Lena Johnson, who led marches and gave fiery speeches, Sarah's role in the fight for justice was quieter, more behind the scenes. But her contribution was no less important. She was one of the few white voices in DeFuniak Springs willing to stand up and say, "This is wrong, and it needs to change."

Over time, Sarah and Lena became close allies, their friendship built on a shared commitment to equality and justice. Together, they worked to organize community meetings, rally support for the desegregation of the lake, and push back against the town elders who sought to keep the status quo intact. It wasn't easy, and there were many moments of doubt and frustration. But through it all, Sarah remained steadfast in her belief that a more inclusive DeFuniak Springs was possible.

In the end, Sarah Whitfield's story is one of quiet determination and moral fortitude. She understood that the fight for equality in DeFuniak Springs was not going to be won overnight. She knew that the deeply entrenched racism of the town elders like Wallace was not going to be undone by a few marches or petitions. But she also knew that change had to start somewhere, and that each step forward—no matter how small—was a victory in itself.

Teacher's have influence in most communities. The Springs was no different. As the weeks and months went by, Sarah's influence began to show in unexpected ways. In her classroom, the seeds of critical thinking she had planted were starting to grow. Some of her students, who had initially been resistant to her teachings about racial equality, were beginning to ask questions. They were starting to see their town in a new light, to question the stories they had been told by their parents and grandparents.

One of her most promising students, a girl named Emily, approached Sarah after class one day.

"Ms. Whitfield, I've been thinking a lot about what you said in class last week, about the civil rights movement. I talked to my grandfather about it, and he got really angry. He said the things you're teaching aren't true. But… I don't know, I feel like there's more to the story than he's telling me. How do I know what's true?"

Sarah smiled softly. This was the kind of question she lived for—evidence that her students were beginning to think for themselves, to question the narratives they had grown up with. "That's a great question, Emily," Sarah said. "And honestly, it's not always easy to know what's true. But one thing

I always tell my students is to listen to multiple perspectives. History is made up of many voices, and sometimes the loudest voices aren't the most honest ones. It's up to us to dig deeper, to find the voices that have been silenced or ignored. And when it comes to race in the South, there are a lot of stories that have been left out of the history books."

Emily nodded, her face thoughtful. "I think I want to learn more. Can you recommend any books?"

Sarah's heart swelled with pride. Moments like this —when she saw her students begin to open their minds and challenge the status quo—were what made the backlash and the isolation worth it. She gave Emily a list of books, from works by civil rights leaders like Martin Luther King Jr. and James Baldwin to historical accounts of Reconstruction and Jim Crow.

It wasn't long before Emily began to share what she was learning with her friends. Soon, a small group of students formed who were eager to dive deeper into the issues Sarah was teaching. They met after school, sometimes in Sarah's classroom and sometimes at local cafés, discussing topics that had once been taboo in DeFuniak Springs. They talked about racism, inequality, and the future of their town. Sarah encouraged them to think critically, to ask hard questions, and most importantly, to act on what they believed.

This small group of students became the next generation of activists in DeFuniak Springs—young people who, like Sarah, were determined to push their town forward, despite the resistance from their elders.

It was no surprise to town folk that the town elders started to push back. But while Sarah was slowly building a movement among her students, the town elders were not sitting idly by. Wallace and his allies were growing increasingly frustrated with the changes they were seeing in the town, and they saw Whitfield as a direct threat. To them, she represented everything wrong with the younger generation—disrespectful of tradition, too eager to embrace ideas from outside, and dangerously sympathetic to the Black community's demands.

At a town meeting, Wallace made no attempt to hide his disdain for Whitfield. "This is our town," he declared, his voice booming across the room. "We built this town. Our fathers and grandfathers fought for it. And now we have people coming in here… outsiders… trying to change things, trying to tell us that everything we believe is wrong. Well, I won't stand for it. And I know many of you won't either."

Though he didn't name Whitfield outright, everyone in the room knew who he was talking about. After the meeting, some of her colleagues at the school began to distance themselves from her, afraid that their association with her might cause trouble. A few even suggested that she should leave town altogether, for her own safety.

But Sarah Whitfield refused to be intimidated. She knew that the backlash was a sign that the work she and Lena were doing was having an effect. If they weren't making progress, the town elders wouldn't be so desperate to stop them.

As the fight to reopen Lake DeFuniak escalated, Sarah became more involved in the activism led by Lena Johnson. She attended protests, helped organize community meetings, and even used her classroom as a space to educate people about the legal battles being fought over desegregation. Lena often leaned on Sarah's knowledge of history, asking her to explain the broader context of their struggle to the community.

One particularly tense evening, Sarah and Lena sat together in the back of a local café, discussing strategy. "We're close, Sarah," Lena said, her voice filled with both determination and exhaustion. "I can feel it. The courts are leaning our way, but Wallace and the elders are going to push back harder than ever. They're not gonna let this lake go without a fight."

Sarah nodded. "I know. But we've come too far to turn back now. The community is waking up. Even some of the white folks are starting to question why the lake has to stay closed."

Lena smiled, though it didn't quite reach her eyes. "That's thanks to you, you know. People listen to you because you're one of them. They're starting to realize that this fight isn't just about Black and White—it's about right and wrong."

Sarah blushed at the praise. "I'm just trying to do what's right, same as you."

As they continued planning their next steps, Sarah couldn't shake the feeling that the town was on the brink of something monumental. The old ways of DeFuniak Springs were crumbling, and though the process was painful and slow… no going back.

But there is always a cost to standing up and this was no different and standing for what was right would come at a cost. One evening, as Sarah was walking home from school, she found a note tucked under the windshield wiper of her car. The message was simple, but chilling: "We don't need troublemakers like you here. Leave, or else."

She stood in the parking lot for a long time, staring at the note. A wave of fear washed over her, but it was quickly replaced by resolve. She knew this was a scare tactic, an attempt to silence her. But Sarah had come too far to be scared off by threats.

She took the note to the local police station, but the officer at the desk gave her a dismissive shrug. "You know how people are around here," he said.

Sarah walked out of the station feeling deflated. She knew that the police weren't going to protect her, not when so many of them shared the same views as the town elders. But she knew she wasn't alone. Lena had faced far worse threats, and if Lena could keep going, so could she.

As the battle over the lake dragged on, Whitfield began to see small but significant changes in the town. More and more people—both Black and white—were joining the movement to reopen the lake. Some of the older white residents who had been staunchly opposed to integration were starting to soften, if only because they were tired of the tension and wanted to move forward.

One afternoon, as she was walking through town, she ran into Emily and her group of friends, who had become some of her most dedicated students.

They were carrying signs, heading to another rally at the lake. The protests did little but helped to build solitary and insure that the issue was not moot and remained in people's minds. "Ms. Whitfield, are you coming?" Emily asked, her face beaming with excitement.

She smiled. "Wouldn't miss it for the world." As she walked with her students toward the lake, Sarah felt a sense of hope that she hadn't felt in a long time. For the first time in years, it felt like Springs might finally be ready to change.

Sarah Whitfield's role in the fight to reopen the Lake was just one chapter in the larger story of DeFuniak Springs' transformation. She represented the new generation of the South—a generation that rejected the racism of the past and sought to build a more inclusive future. Though her path was fraught with challenges, Sarah remained steadfast in her belief that the town could change, that the people of DeFuniak Springs could learn from their history and move forward together.

And though Wallace and the town elders would continue to resist, Sarah knew that the future belonged to those who were willing to fight for justice and equality. She wasn't just teaching her students history—she was helping them write a brand new one.

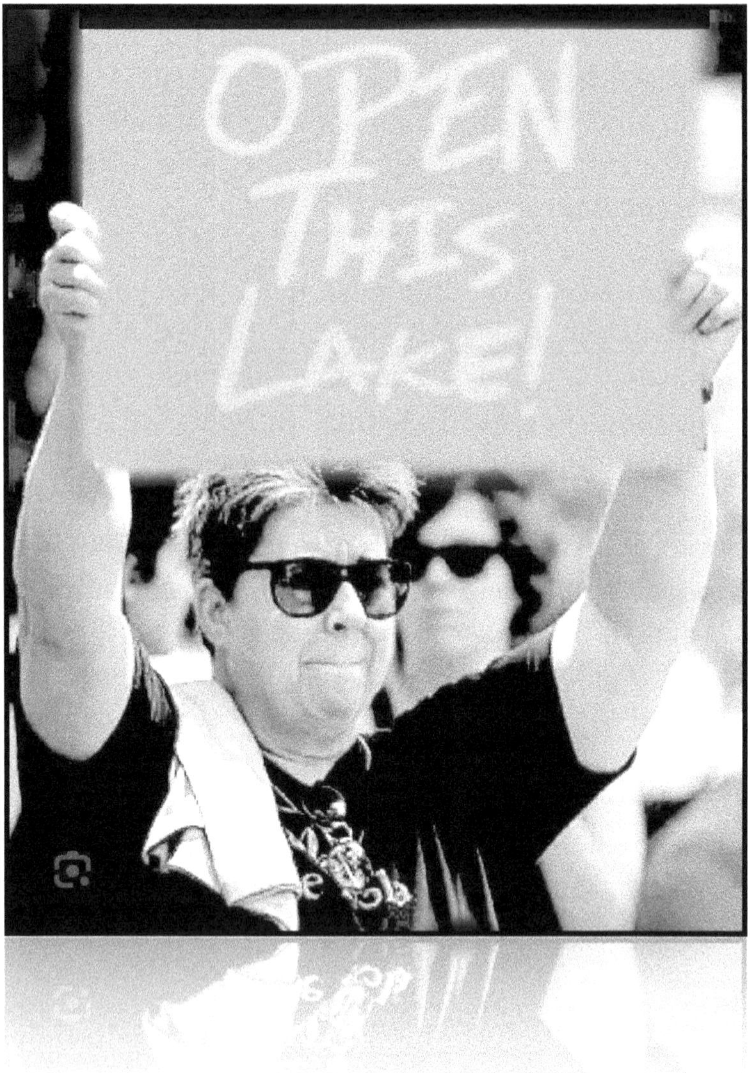
OPEN
THIS
LAKE!

CHAPTER 7

The Lake Reopens
Healing Waters?

If you care to define the South as a poor, rural region with lousy race relations, that South survives only in geographical shreds and patches and most Southerners don't live there any more.
Sociologist John Shelton Reed

Lena walked into the mayor's office with a determined stride, her heart pounding in her chest but her face a mask of calm. Mayor Wallace sat behind his large oak desk, the smell of cigar smoke lingering in the room, mingling with the scent of old leather and varnish. His eyes flicked up to meet hers, hard and cold, as if her mere presence was an inconvenience. He didn't offer her a seat.

"Miss Johnson," he said, leaning back in his chair and folding his hands over his stomach. "To what do I owe this… visit?"

Lena didn't waste any time. "I'm here about the lake, Mayor Wallace. You know damn well why it was shut down. We've been patient long enough."

Wallace raised an eyebrow, his expression one of mock surprise. "The lake? It's closed for maintenance, Miss Johnson. You know that. Safety concerns." he said with a smirk.

"That's bullshit, and we both know it," Lena snapped, stepping forward, her hands clenched into fists at her sides. She hadn't come here to mince words. "It's been closed ever since we tried to use it. Don't act like it's a coincidence."

The mayor's smile didn't reach his eyes. "I think you're overestimating your influence, Lena. The lake is closed for the good of the town. Tensions are high right now. I'm just trying to keep things from getting… out of hand."

"You're trying to keep things exactly the way they've always been," she shot back. "We've been shut out of that lake for years, and now you'd rather close it down entirely than let us near it. You can't just erase us, Mr. Mayor."

Wallace's smile faded, his jaw tightening as he sat up straighter in his chair. "You people have always had your place, Miss Johnson. You come in here, stirring up trouble, thinking you can change things overnight. But this isn't Birmingham, or Washington. This is Walton County. And things aren't going to change just because you throw a little tantrum."

Lena felt a surge of anger rise in her throat, but she swallowed it down. She wouldn't give him the satisfaction of seeing her lose control. "We're not asking for anything more than what's rightfully ours. This lake belongs to everyone, not just white folks. We've waited long enough, and we're done waiting. The time has come!"

The mayor stood up slowly, his tall frame casting a shadow over the room as he leaned over the desk, his hands pressing down on the surface. His voice lowered, his tone menacing. "You think you can come in here, make demands, and I'll just roll over? You don't understand how this town works. I run this place. I decide what happens here, and as long as I'm sitting in this chair, there's not a damn thing you or anyone else can do to change that."

Lena held her ground, her chin lifting in defiance. "You're wrong, Wallace. Things are already changing, whether you like it or not. You can close the lake, the sheriff to arrest us, but we're not going away and we're not scared of you anymore."

Wallace's eyes narrowed, his face flushed with barely contained rage. "You ought to be scared. You don't know the kind of people you're dealing with, Lena. There are men in this town who won't hesitate to do what's necessary to keep things in order in our town, y'all should remember that."

"Are you threatening me?" Lena asked, her voice steady but cold. And looking directly into his eyes.

The mayor leaned back, a smirk tugging at the corner of his mouth. "I don't make threats, Miss Johnson I don't need ta. I is just reminding you of the way things are. And the way they will stay."

Lena shook her head, her voice rising with quiet conviction. "You can't stop this. You can fight it, but it's bigger than you. Bigger than me. The world is changing, Mr. Wallace, and time is running out for you and folks who think like you."

For a moment, neither of them spoke. The air between them crackled with tension, the unspoken truth hanging in the space like a sword waiting to drop. Wallace's hand clenched into a fist on the desk, his knuckles turning white.

"I'd be careful if I were you, Lena," Wallace said finally, his voice low and venomous. "You've already caused enough trouble. I'd hate to see anything happen to you or your family."

Lena's lips pressed into a thin line, her pulse pounding in her ears, but she didn't flinch. She stared at him, her eyes burning with defiance. "You don't scare me, Mayor. And you won't scare us into silence… ever. Those days are over!"

With that, she turned on her heel and walked out of the office, the door slamming shut behind her with a finality that echoed in the empty hallway.

It was 2017 and Lena Johnson stood at the edge of Lake DeFuniak, her heart racing with a mix of excitement and disbelief. It was a bright Saturday morning, the sun casting shimmering reflections across the water's surface, each ripple a reminder of the countless dreams deferred over decades of exclusion. Fifty-seven years of segregation had ended with a single stroke of a pen, and now, for the first time, Black residents were allowed to swim in the lake that had been their ancestral playground—now reclaimed after years of oppression and waiting.

The town buzzed with anticipation as members of the community began to gather. Lena, now in her forties, had once been the young activist leading the charge against injustice. As a teenager, she had marched for civil rights, faced down angry crowds, and fought for change that felt painfully slow. Today, she was both a leader and a witness to history that had refused to be forgotten, even in the face of overwhelming resistance.

"Look at them," Lena said, glancing over at the gathering crowd, her voice trembling with emotion. Friends, family, and neighbors had come to witness this momentous occasion. The air was thick with anticipation and nostalgia, a mix of laughter and nervous chatter as people settled on the grass, some with picnic baskets and coolers, ready to celebrate what felt like a second chance.

As Lena stepped forward, she took a deep breath, inhaling the scent of pine and lake water. "We're doing this for everyone who fought before us," she said, raising her voice to call the crowd's attention. "For those who dreamed of swimming here, for those who stood against the tide of hate and exclusion. Today, we reclaim this lake!"

A round of applause broke out, followed by cheers that echoed through the trees. The laughter of children filled the air, a beautiful melody that blended seamlessly with the gentle lapping of water against the shore. The once-hallowed grounds of segregation were now a space of unity, where everyone—regardless of color—could gather and celebrate their freedom.

Lena felt a surge of pride wash over her as she watched the diverse crowd. There were families who had lived in DeFuniak Springs for generations, and there were newcomers who had come to see what all the excitement was about. Today, they were all joined in purpose.

"Are ya ready?" a familiar voice called from behind her. It was Jimmy Bedford, her longtime ally and friend. His fiery passion for social justice had been unwavering since their early days of activism. Though he had faced his own challenges, he had stood by Lena, challenging the prejudices of his own community and advocating for a more inclusive future.

"Ready as I'll ever be!" Lena replied, turning to face him, a broad smile breaking across her face. Jimmy's eyes shone with excitement, reflecting the beauty of the day. "Let's show them what it means to be free," he said, gesturing toward the water.

With a nod, Lena led the charge. As they marched toward the water, she could feel the pulse of the crowd behind her, a united front of Black and White residents ready to embrace a new beginning. The closer they got to the water's edge, the more the cheers grew louder. It was a sound that had been silenced for far too long.

"On the count of three!" Lena shouted, lifting her arms as she reached the shoreline. "One! Two! Three!" Lena dove in, the coolness enveloping her like a loving embrace.

They surged forward, a wave of joyous humanity as they splashed into the lake, the water glistening like diamonds around them.. It was a feeling she had longed for, one she had watched from the sidelines for years. As she surfaced, laughter erupted all around her, the sound reverberating against the banks of the lake, drowning out the echoes of the past.

Nearby, children squealed with delight, their small bodies launching into the water, unburdened by the history that had once kept them at bay. Parents joined in, some splashing water toward one another, while others floated lazily in the shallows, reveling in their newfound freedom. Lena swam deeper, relishing the feeling of liberation as the water danced around her, washing away the weight of decades of exclusion.

As Lena floated on her back, she looked up at the bright blue sky, the sun warming her skin. She closed her eyes, allowing herself to drift away from the pain of the past and embrace the joy of the present. This was more than just a swim; it was a victory for all the voices that had been silenced, for the dreams that had been postponed.

When she finally opened her eyes, she saw Jimmy standing at the water's edge, his arm raised high in celebration. She smiled back at him, knowing that their fight had not been in vain. This was their moment—a testament to the strength of their community, a reminder that change was not only possible, but inevitable.

As the day unfolded, stories were shared and memories created. People who had lived in fear for so long now laughed freely, their voices mingling with the rustling leaves. It was a moment that felt both monumental and intimate, a reminder of everything they had fought for and everything they had yet to achieve.

Lena knew that the road ahead would still be fraught with challenges; the scars of the past would not disappear overnight. But as she watched her neighbors—young and old—finding joy in the water, she felt a glimmer of hope. The lake had reopened, and with it, a new chapter for DeFuniak Springs began.

Today, the waters of Lake DeFuniak sparkled not just with sunlight, but with the promise of unity, healing, and a brighter future. As she splashed back toward the shore, Lena understood that this was just the beginning, a long-awaited reunion with a place that had always belonged to them. They were not just reclaiming the lake; they were reclaiming their dignity, their rights, and their community. And together, they would continue to push for change, one joyous splash at a time.

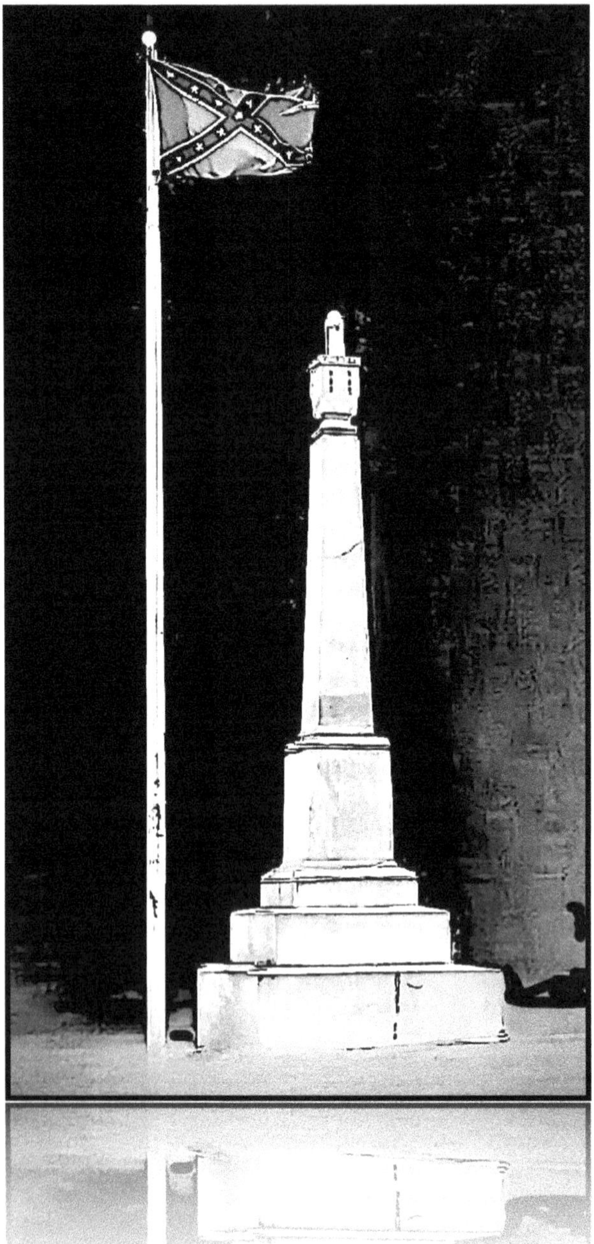

CHAPTER 8

Flag Fight
A Symbol of Hate or Culture?

You can't separate peace from freedom because no one can be at peace unless he has his freedom.
Malcolm X

Lena Johnson sat at the weathered wooden table in her father's kitchen, flipping through old family photos spread out before her. Elijah was in the backyard, trimming the grass along the fence, his usual Saturday ritual. But today, Lena felt the weight of something more than family history resting on her shoulders. Today, the town of DeFuniak Springs would gather in the square to decide the fate of the Confederate flag that had flown outside the courthouse for as long as she could remember.

The same flag that had always been there, fluttering indifferently in the Florida heat, a silent symbol of a past that some called heritage and others called hate. DeFuniak Springs is home to one of the second oldest Confederate monuments in the country and the first one in the state of Florida. The Confederate monument was erected in 1871 on the old courthouse grounds in Valley Church, then moved to a new courthouse site in

Eucheeanna and finally moved to DeFuniak Springs when this courthouse was built. It was erected in memory of the county's war dead and was reportedly the first such monument built. A Confederate battle flag was erected next to the monument on the Walton County courthouse lawn in April 1964 according to the DeFuniak Herald/Beach Breeze newspaper. On July 28, 2015, the Walton County Board of County Commissioners voted to replace the Confederate battle flag with the first national flag of the Confederate States of America. Adopted in 1861, the flag known as the 'Stars and Bars' was flown over the dome of the first Confederate Capitol in Montgomery, Ala.

Many felt and feel that the county has simply gone from a symbol of segregation to a symbol of slavery. Many organization including the NAACP had warned of the potential economic impact a decision to keep the Confederate flag flying could have on the county. The new county flag is seen by others as a fair compromise… but not by very much.

Lena sighed, rubbing her temples, feeling the pressure of the past week bearing down on her. It had been a hell of a fight just to get the town council to put the removal of the flag on the agenda. Resistance was fierce, particularly from the older, white residents of Walton County who saw the flag as a relic of their identity.

"We've been fighting this for too long," she muttered under her breath, pushing away the photos. The one that caught her eye was of her grandmother, standing proudly beside a sign for the Colored School in the 1950s, back when segregation was law and the South was a different world. Lena knew all too well that not much had changed since then, not in the ways that mattered.

Her phone buzzed on the table. A text from Marsha. You ready?

Lena typed back quickly: "Heading out now."

She stood and glanced out the window at her father, his strong hands moving steadily with the clippers. He was slower than he used to be, but he'd always been like that—methodical, deliberate in everything he did. For him, the fight wasn't new. It was a continuation of what his parents and grandparents had fought for. But Lena felt something different this time, a kind of urgency that wasn't there before. The battle for the flag was a line in the sand—a battle for the soul of the town.

She stepped outside, the humidity wrapping around her like a second skin.

"Elijah, you want to come to the square?" she asked, knowing the answer already.

Her father paused and looked up, wiping the sweat from his brow. His face was lined with age, his dark skin glistening in the late morning sun. "I'll be there when it's done," he said. "That's your fight now."

Lena nodded, understanding what he meant. He had fought his battles, but now it was her turn. She kissed him on the cheek and headed for her car, the drive into town feeling heavier than usual.

The square was already packed when Lena arrived. A mix of young activists, church leaders, and families had gathered on one side of the courthouse, holding signs that read, *'Take It Down!'* and *'Our Heritage Is Equality'*. On the other side, a smaller but louder group had formed, waving Confederate flags of their own, some dressed in shirts emblazoned with slogans like, The South Will Rise Again and Heritage Not Hate.

Lena found Marsha near the courthouse steps, holding a clipboard and barking orders into her phone.

"Lena, thank God you're here," Marsha said, lowering the phone and hugging her. "It's crazy already."

"I can see that," Lena said, eyeing the Confederate flag supporters across the square. Some of them had gathered at the base of the monument that honored Confederate soldiers—a stone obelisk that had stood in the center of DeFuniak Springs for over a century. The tension in the air was thick, and Lena could feel it in her bones.

"I don't know if we're going to get through to them today," Marsha said, her voice tight with frustration. "The council's divided, and you know the mayor—he's not exactly on our side."

Mayor Wallace had been one of the most vocal opponents of removing the flag. To him, and to many like him, the flag represented a connection to the past, to the ancestors who had fought for the Confederacy. To people like Lena and Marsha, it was a symbol of oppression, of the systemic racism that still lingered in Walton County.

"They have to listen to us," Lena said firmly. "This is 2017. How much longer can they hide behind 'heritage' as an excuse?"

Marsha nodded. "We'll see. The council meeting starts in ten minutes."

As they made their way to the courthouse steps, Lena noticed the tension simmering between the two groups. A few men on the other side glared at her as she passed, their eyes hard and unyielding. She recognized some of them from around town—men she'd gone to school with, who'd grown up in the same streets and neighborhoods, but whose lives had taken vastly different paths. They were people who clung to a version of Walton County that no longer existed, or at least, didn't have to.

The doors to the courthouse opened, and the crowd began to file in. Lena took a seat near the front with Marsha, their eyes focused on the row of council members seated behind a long wooden table. Mayor , sitting at the center, gave a perfunctory smile as the room filled, but there was no mistaking the tension in his jaw. He knew what this meeting represented.

The flag was on trial there was no doubt it. The council went through the usual motions— approving minutes, discussing minor issues—but the room was humming with anticipation for the final agenda item. When it finally came time to discuss the flag, the mayor cleared his throat and spoke into the microphone.

"All right, folks," he said. "We're here today to discuss the possibility of removing the Confederate flag from public display on county property. We'll hear from both sides, but let me remind everyone to remain civil. This is a respectful debate."

Respectful, Lena thought. There was nothing respectful about the hatred that flag represented.

The first to speak was Bill Reed, one of the leading voices of the pro-flag faction. A man in his sixties with a broad, ruddy face, he stepped to the microphone with a confidence that made Lena's stomach churn.

"The Confederate flag is part of our history," Reed began, his voice carrying easily through the room. "My great-granddaddy fought for the South in the War Between the States. He wasn't fighting for slavery; he was fighting for his home, for his way of life. That flag is a symbol sacrifice, and of the heritage that made this country what it is today."

Lena clenched her fists under the table. Reed's words were the same ones she'd heard her entire life, a narrative that sanitized the horrors of slavery and the oppression that followed. But she knew it would resonate with many in this room, especially the older, white council members.

Reed continued. "Taking down that flag won't change history. It won't erase the fact that the South was built on hard work and sacrifice. We can't just tear down everything that reminds us of who we are."

Lena couldn't help but notice the way Reed's eyes flicked toward the Black members of the audience as he said "who we are," as if he were drawing a line in the sand.

When he finished, a smattering of applause came from the Confederate flag supporters in the back.

Lena's heart raced as she stood up, her legs slightly unsteady beneath her. It was her turn to speak.

As she approached the podium, she felt the weight of the room's gaze on her, both supportive and hostile. She had grown up in this town, gone to school with many of these people, and yet at this moment, she felt like a stranger.

"My name is Lena Johnson," she began, her voice clear. "I'm from DeFuniak Springs, just like most of you. I grew up seeing that flag outside the courthouse every day. And every time I saw it, I was reminded that this town wasn't built for me. It wasn't built for people who look like me, whose ancestors were enslaved under that flag." She paused, letting the words settle in. A hush had fallen over the room, the tension thick as the Florida summer air.

"I know some of you see that flag as history. But for many of us, it's a symbol of hate, of exclusion. It represents a past that glorified the oppression of Black people, a past that this town—this country—has been trying to move beyond. We can't celebrate a history that enslaved and dehumanized so many of our ancestors."

Her voice grew stronger. "Removing the flag isn't about erasing history. It's about acknowledging that this history hurt people. It's about recognizing that symbols of hate have no place on public buildings where everyone—Black, white, and everything in between—is supposed to feel equal."

A murmur ran through the crowd, but Lena pressed on. "We've made progress in this town. But leaving that flag up there is a message. It's a message that the past still rules the present, that the voices of those who were oppressed still don't matter. It's time to take it down."

She stepped back from the microphone, her heart pounding. A wave of silence followed her words, and then, slowly, applause began to build. Marsha grabbed her hand, squeezing it tight, as more people stood up, clapping, nodding. But not everyone. Across the room, a wall of stony faces remained, arms crossed with jaws set in defiance.

Mayor shifted in his seat, his face unreadable. When the applause died down, he cleared his throat again.

"We've heard both sides," he said, looking uncomfortable. "Maybe Now, it's time to make a decision y'all."

The summer heat hung heavy over Walton County, turning the air thick and oppressive. Outside the courthouse, the Confederate flag flapped lazily in the breeze, its faded red fabric stark against the bright blue sky. It had been there for as long as anyone could remember, a quiet, constant reminder of the past. For years, people had driven by it, some barely noticing, others bristling at the sight of it but saying nothing. But now, in 2020, that was changing, slowly but surly.

It started with the protests. First, they were small—dozens of people, mostly younger, carrying signs that read "No More Hate" and "Take It Down." Some days, there were only a handful of them, standing in the shadow of the courthouse, their voices loud against the backdrop of history. But their numbers grew as national outrage over racial injustice spread. The deaths of George Floyd, Breonna Taylor, and Ahmaud Arbery had lit a fire across the country, and that fire had reached Walton County.

Malaysia Jackson had been there for the first protest. At seventy-five, her legs were slower, her breath shorter, but her spirit was as fierce as ever. She had stood in the same spot forty years earlier, fighting for the right to vote without intimidation, to attend integrated schools, to simply live with dignity. And now she was back, her hand gripping a wooden sign, her eyes fixed on that flag.

Her granddaughter Imani stood beside her, holding her own sign that read: "The Past Is Over. Take It Down." Imani's eyes burned with the same determination Malaysia had once carried, but now her fight was different—more visible, more public. The world was watching Walton County.

The courthouse steps were crowded that day, as more protesters gathered under the relentless sun. There were speeches—some impassioned, others weary from years of trying to convince the town that the flag didn't represent heritage, but hate. Mayor Tom Wallace, grandson of the infamous Walton Wallace who had fiercely defended segregation in the 1960s, had been at the center of the controversy. He was a man steeped in tradition, one who believed that removing the flag was erasing history, not confronting it. He had resisted every call to take it down, claiming it was a part of Southern heritage that deserved to remain.

"Heritage, not hate," he had said during a city council meeting earlier that month, his voice calm but resolute. "The Confederate flag is a symbol of where we come from. It's not about racism, it's about honoring the people who fought for their land and our culture," he said.

But those words had done nothing to quell the rising anger. For people like Malaysia and Imani, and for much of the Black community in Walton County, the flag wasn't a symbol of heritage. It was a reminder of the violence and oppression that had been inflicted on their ancestors. To them, the flag didn't represent pride—it represented pain.

The fight had escalated quickly. What had started as peaceful protests grew louder and more contentious. Groups of counter-protesters, mostly white men and women from the surrounding rural areas, began showing up, waving their own Confederate flags and shouting at the protesters to "leave the past alone."

"Leave our history alone!" a man shouted at Malaysia during one of the protests. He was younger than her, his face twisted in anger as he waved his flag defiantly. "You're trying to destroy everything that makes us who we are!"

Malaysia had simply looked at him, her eyes steady, her voice calm. "I'm not trying to destroy history. I'm makin' sure we don't repeat it."

The tension in town was noticeable. City council meetings became battlegrounds, where lines were drawn between those who wanted to keep the flag flying and those who wanted to see it gone. For every person who stood up in support of taking it down, there was another who clung to it with a fierceness that felt, to Malaysia, like desperation.

Imani had been vocal at those meetings, her voice shaking with emotion as she spoke about what the flag meant to her generation. "I don't care what it meant to people in the past," she had said at one meeting. "All I know is that when I see it, I feel like I don't belong here. Like this town doesn't want me. That's not a heritage worth preserving."
The council had listened, but there had been no decision. They had delayed, pushed the vote back, claiming they needed more time to consider all sides. But Malaysia knew what that really meant—they were afraid. Afraid of angering the old guard, afraid of admitting that the town needed to change.

It was at the final council meeting of the summer, when tempers were at their highest, that the real confrontation came. The room was packed—Black families, young white activists, older men in denim jackets with Confederate patches sewn into the fabric, their faces red with anger. The tension was thick enough to cut with a knife.

Mayor Wallace stood at the front of the room, his face stern, his hands gripping the podium. He had never wavered in his defense of the flag, but even he looked wearied by the fight. The pressure was mounting, and the decision was inevitable. But no one knew which way it would go.

"I know this is an emotional issue for many people," the mayor began, his voice slow and deliberate. "And I understand both sides. But we must remember that this flag has flown over this courthouse for decades. It's part of who we are."

"That flag doesn't represent who we are now," a voice called from the back of the room. It was Jimmy Bedford, a white man who had moved to Walton County in the 1980s and had become an unlikely ally to the Black community. "It represents who we were—who we shouldn't be anymore."

The room erupted in applause and angry shouts, the noise deafening as the two sides clashed, their voices filling the small space. Malaysia watched as the mayor's face tightened, his grip on the podium hardening.

"We can't just erase history," Mayor Wallace said, raising his voice to be heard over the din. "We have to honor it."

Imani stood up then, her voice cutting through the noise like a knife. "Taking down that flag isn't erasing history—it's acknowledging that our history is complicated, and not something to be proud of. You're not erasing it by taking it down—you're letting us move forward."

There was a brief silence, and for a moment, it seemed like the mayor might waver. But then the crowd surged again, the tension boiling over. It wasn't just about the flag—it was about what it symbolized. The old Walton County, clinging to its

Confederate past, and the new one, fighting to redefine itself.

After what felt like hours, the council finally took the vote. Malaysia held her breath, her hands clenched in her lap. Imani stood beside her, her body taut with anticipation.

The vote was 4-3 in favor of taking the flag down.

The room erupted again, this time in a mix of cheers and boos. The counter-protesters stormed out, their faces red with fury, while the others hugged and cried, their joy tinged with relief. It wasn't the end of the fight, Malaysia knew. There would be more resistance, more attempts to cling to the past. But for the first time, it felt like Walton County was moving forward. But not by much as a compromise the country put up a different flag from the confederacy.

As she and Imani walked out of the courthouse that evening, the flag still flapping in the warm summer breeze for now, Malaysia looked up at the courthouse and smiled. It was a small victory, but a victory nonetheless.

"That damn flag's coming down," she whispered, more to herself than to anyone else. "We're finally moving on."

The summer night was thick with humidity as Malaysia and Imani stepped out of the courthouse, the flag still hanging stubbornly from its pole, as if clinging to its place in the sky. Even though the vote had gone in their favor, the sight of that flag flapping against the backdrop of the old courthouse felt like a taunt. But the vote had been cast. It would come down in time.

Imani's eyes burned with a fierce sense of victory, but Malaysia could see the exhaustion beneath it. The fight had been long and hard, but they had won—at least, this battle.

"They're going to fight it, you know," Imani said as they walked down the courthouse steps, her voice laced with both triumph and wariness. "They'll appeal it, they'll rally the people who wanted it to stay. This isn't over."

Malaysia nodded, knowing full well that Imani was right. "It's never over," she replied, her voice

softer now, reflecting the weariness of a lifetime of struggle. "Not as long as there are people who believe in that flag. But tonight, we won and it is something important. Something that will help."
Imani turned toward her grandmother, eyes searching Malaysia's face for more than just wisdom. "You think it'll actually come down? For good, I mean?"

Malaysia stopped walking and looked at the courthouse one last time, the red of the Confederate flag almost ghostly under the moonlight. She sighed. "It has to. Maybe not tomorrow, maybe not without more protests or fights. But it's coming down... because it's time."

They continued walking in silence, the streets of DeFuniak Springs quieter now, the tension that had filled the air earlier that day easing into the evening calm. Despite the victory, Malaysia couldn't help but think about all the things that flag still represented, even after its removal was voted for. The wounds it had left in this town were deep, the scars etched into the memories of people like her who had lived through the worst of it.

As they neared Malaysia's house, Imani stopped, turning to face her grandmother once more. Her face was illuminated by the porch light, her eyes filled with both determination and doubt. "Do you think... do you think this really changes anything?" she asked, her voice softer now. "I mean, I'm glad we won, but there's still so much hate. It's like it's just hiding, waiting for the next thing to fight over."

Malaysia looked at her granddaughter and saw herself at that age—young, passionate, and desperate for change to come faster than it ever did. She reached out, taking Imani's hand in her own. "Baby, change is slow. You know that. I've been fighting for a long time, and there were days when I didn't think anything would get better. But we're standing here, together, fighting side by side, because things did change. Not everything, not all at once, but enough to make a difference. This fight, this flag—it's just one step."

Imani nodded, her eyes misting, "I just don't want to be fighting this same battle when I'm your age."

"You won't be," Malaysia said firmly. "You'll have your own battles, new ones. But you won't be fighting the same fight and that's progress."

The next day, the courthouse lawn was quieter than it had been in weeks. A few news cameras were stationed near the entrance, hoping to catch footage of the flag finally coming down. A small crowd of supporters had gathered, holding signs and banners that read "Progress, Not Pride" and "Take It Down." But across the street, a group of counter-protesters had formed, their faces defiant, their own Confederate flags waving in the air, symbols of a past they refused to let go of.

Imani and Malaysia stood among the supporters, watching as city workers approached the flagpole. For a moment, it seemed like time had stopped, the crowd holding its breath as the workers reached up to unhook the Confederate flag. There was a tension in the air, as if the very fabric of the town was being pulled in two directions—one toward the future, one anchored in the past.

As the flag began to lower, a cheer erupted from the supporters, a mix of relief and joy. But across the street, the counter-protesters booed and jeered, their anger palpable. One man, his face flushed with rage, yelled, "You're destroying our history! You're tearing down our heritage!"

Imani's jaw clenched as she heard the words, her hands tightening into fists. Malaysia placed a calming hand on her arm. "Let it go, baby. Don't let them take this moment from you."

The flag hit the ground, and for a brief moment, the world felt like it had shifted. But as the workers folded the fabric and carried it inside the courthouse, Malaysia knew the real fight was far from over. The removal of the flag was symbolic, yes—but symbols carried power, and there were those in Walton County who would fight tooth and nail to restore what they believed had been taken from them.

As the crowd began to disperse, Imani turned to her grandmother, her expression one of quiet determination. "It's a start," she said softly.

Malaysia smiled with pride. "Yes, indeed it is."

In the days and weeks that followed, the town of DeFuniak Springs adjusted to life without the Confederate flag flying over its courthouse. The conversations didn't stop. In fact, in many ways, they intensified. The counter-protesters didn't go away—they organized rallies of their own, calling for the flag to be reinstated, claiming that their heritage was being erased. Some locals began to publicly question the vote, suggesting it might have been rushed, calling for "further discussions."

But the flag didn't go back up. And for the first time in a long time, Malaysia felt like the town was moving in the right direction. The scars were still there—decades of racial division couldn't be undone with the removal of a flag. But as Malaysia watched the younger generation—Imani and her friends—she felt hope. They were different. They didn't accept the excuses of tradition and heritage as reasons to perpetuate hate. They wanted something better, something more just. And they were willing to fight for it.

As she sat on her porch one evening, watching the sun set over the small town she had called home for so many years, Malaysia knew there would always be resistance. The legacy of the past was strong in Walton County, but so was the will to change. The flag had come down, and it was just the beginning.

For the first time in a long time, she believed that the future of the County might finally be different. It might finally belong to everyone.

But sitting on the Courthouse lawn is the second oldest Confederate monument in the country and it represents different things to different people.

"All citizens of Walton County access the courthouse for many reasons and a Confederate flag flying at the steps is a symbol of white supremacy," said Margie Jordan, a former chairwoman of the Walton County Democratic Party. "In light of a national crisis of rising racism, bigotry, separatism, and unprecedented division in our country… it's time for healing," said Jordan.

Stephen McBroom considers himself a Walton County Heritage volunteer and believes the statue represents nothing other than history."This is my heritage, this is the history of this town. I love this town, I was born here. I'm fourth generation in this county," he said. "I have a lot invested here."

"All through the nation, these monuments to hatred, oppression, and racism are being taken down and in our area, we have our county government represented by a Confederate flag," said Doctor Carolynn Zonia, who wants to see the monument and flag removed and was interviewed on local TV.

"Everything that happened in Charlottesville was all about hate, not about history or heritage and that's what we are all about here in Walton County. It's about our heritage because we have a lot to brag about in DeFuniak Springs and we're proud of it," said McBroom.

"The flying of the Confederate flag at our county courthouse in DeFuniak Springs was a contentious

When Walton County took down the Confederate 'Stars and Bars' Battle Flag it simply substituted the less known flag of the treasonous Confederate States of America, with the seven stars signifying the first seven Confederate states.

issue for many years. There is a small but loud and angry group of Confederate sympathizers that use anger and threats to keep down any opposition," said Jordan.

But McBroom said in the media at the time that it needs to stay right where it is. "On the side of the monument, there is an inscription that says, 'In memory of the Florida soldiers that served the Confederacy' and that's the whole reason it should stay," he stated. Others felt the exact opposite. The controversy over the Confederate monuments and flags weren't just dividing the country, but also the local people of DeFuniak Springs.

"White supremacists want these monuments and flags flying and it's time for good people to stand up and say monuments to hatred are no longer welcome," Zonia said.

"The people that want to move it or tear it down, they're not from here. There are very few of them and they have no heritage and they want to focus in on how they feel about it. Well, this is how I feel about it," McBroom expressed. "Leave it be!"

Zonia believes we can still teach history without celebrating it through these monuments. "Together we are progress. We can change the world together," she stated. "I believe that."

"I feel like if we could sit down and talk reasonably about history and not focus in on

A summer carriage ride around the 'whites only' lake

racism or hate or anything like that, but just history and heritage maybe people could come to a better understanding," added McBroom. "One thing I've seen is a national trend. If one thing comes down they aren't satisfied. They want another thing and then we have other monuments for the world war veterans, where does it end?"

The final 'compromise' of flying the seven star Confederate States of America flag is still seen by most as a slap in the face and a salute to treason. It still flies above government buildings today.

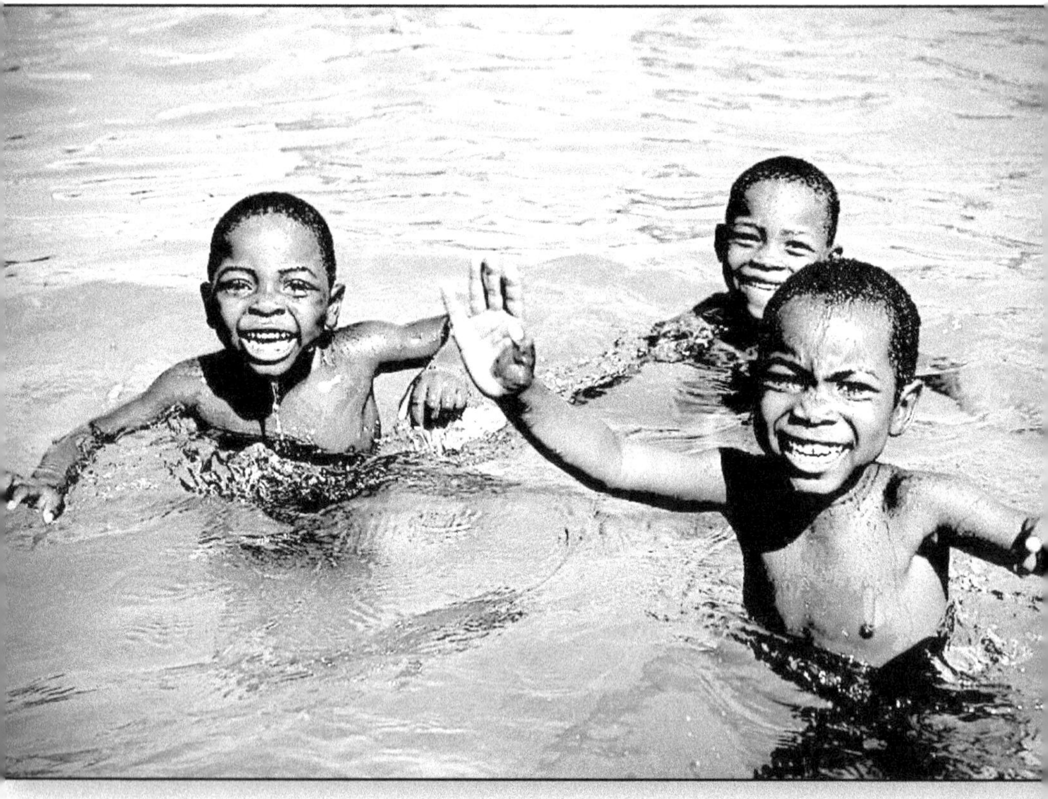

CHAPTER 9

Reflections of Change
A New South?

Hate cannot drive out hate; only love can do that
Martin Luther King, Jr

Jim Crow is alive and it's dressed in a Brooks Brothers suit instead of a white robe!
Myrlie Evers-Williams

The gentle lapping of water against the shore of Lake DeFuniak filled the warm afternoon air as Malaysia Jackson sat on the park bench, shaded by an old oak tree. She looked out at the lake—once a symbol of division, now a gathering place for families, a space where children of all races played without a second thought. The scene was peaceful, but in Malaysia's heart, it stirred memories of a different time. Not all the memories were pleasant.

At seventy-three, she had seen more change than she once thought possible. Raised in the heart of The Springs, she remembered the days when the lake was a place where she and others like her were not welcome. It had been a long journey from the 1960s, when the struggle for civil rights was met with anger and violence, to this moment where she could sit here, undisturbed, watching children laugh and run freely on land that had once been marked by invisible lines of segregation.

She smiled faintly, her wrinkled hands folded in her lap. Time had given her a kind of clarity she hadn't always possessed—an understanding that the fight for justice, for equality, had never truly ended. The scars of the past were still there, visible in the old structures that stood, in the quiet whispers that sometimes surfaced in the grocery store, or the tight-lipped glances exchanged when the town's history was discussed. Yet, beneath it all, under the hate and rhetoric… she saw hope.

The future belonged to those children playing by the water's edge. Black, white, Hispanic, Asian—it didn't matter to them. They were growing up in a new world, one where they didn't have to carry the same burdens as their parents or grandparents. Malaysia knew that didn't mean the world was perfect—far from it. Racism still existed, but it had become more subtle, more covert. Still, the young people were better equipped now. They were more aware, more willing to talk about the divides that had once been unspeakable.

She thought back to her younger self, when she had marched through the streets of DeFuniak Springs, demanding the right to sit at a counter, to vote without harassment, to live with dignity. There had been so much anger then, so much fear —on both sides. The struggle had been real and painful, but without it, they wouldn't be here today. The lake wouldn't be open to everyone. The town would be changing, slowly but surely.

Her granddaughter, Imani, was one of those children she had fought for. At sixteen, Imani was bright, ambitious, and unafraid to speak her mind. She didn't carry the same fear Malaysia had in her youth. Imani moved through the world with a confidence that was the result of a lifetime of progress, but Malaysia worried about her too. The world wasn't as safe as it seemed, and racism had a way of reinventing itself.

Still, Malaysia was proud of what her town had become. The Confederate flag had come down from the courthouse, a small but significant victory. The town had seen a wave of new businesses, people from different cultures setting up shop, bringing a new flavor to the streets. There were more opportunities for young people now than there had been when Malaysia was a girl. The schools had improved, and while Walton County remained conservative, there was a quiet openness creeping in, a slow embrace of diversity.

"Grandma, what're you thinking about?" Imani's voice cut through her reverie.

Malaysia turned to see her granddaughter sitting beside her, legs crossed beneath her on the bench, her curly hair spilling out from under a brightly patterned scarf. Imani's eyes, filled with curiosity and energy, mirrored the youth Malaysia once had, but the world Imani was inheriting was both different and the same.

"Just thinking about how far we've come," Malaysia replied softly, her voice steady. "And how far we've still got to go."

Imani nodded. "Do ya think things will really change, though? I mean, I see the way people talk about race sometimes, like they think it's all better now. But I still feel it, you know? When I'm out with friends people still look at us a certain way."

Malaysia sighed. She had hoped her grandchildren wouldn't have to carry that same burden, but the world wasn't perfect. "It'll take time, baby. Change is slow. Too slow sometimes. But look around you—this lake, these families. That didn't happen overnight. Your mother and I didn't grow up in a world where we could sit here together, looking at a lake that was open to us."

Imani glanced out at the water, watching the sunlight dance across the surface. "Yeah, I guess you're right. But what if people don't want to change? What if we're always stuck with this?"

"There will always be people who want to hold on to the past," Malaysia said. "That's true no matter where you go. But that doesn't mean we stop trying. You're the future of this town, Imani. You and your friends. You've got voices that need to be heard. And whether you see it or not, you're already changing things just by being here, by demanding more."

Imani leaned back, a thoughtful expression on her face. "I hope so. Sometimes it feels like things are better, but it's hard to trust it, you know? I love this town, but it's like there's always something just under the surface."

Malaysia nodded, understanding all too well. "Those feelings are real. We've still got work to do, and those scars you feel—they run deep. But scars mean we've healed some, too. We've survived, and we're still here, still fighting."
She paused, looking out at the lake again. "But I believe in this place. It's not perfect, but it's home. And I believe in your generation. You're going to make sure that the changes stick—that they're real, not just surface-level. You'll keep pushing for better, and you won't let people forget what's been done to get here."

Imani smiled faintly, nodding in agreement. "Yeah, we will. It just feels like a lot sometimes. Like we're always having to fight."

"It is a lot," Malaysia admitted. "But you've got people beside you. You've got your family, your friends, this community. And you've got the history of those who came before you. Don't forget that. You're standing on the shoulders of a lot of strong people who paved the way."

As they sat in silence for a moment, the breeze carrying the scent of jasmine from the nearby gardens, Malaysia felt a quiet peace settle over her. The town had changed, yes, but there was still so much more to be done. The divisions, though no longer overt, still lingered in hushed conversations and private thoughts. Yet, the hope that this new generation—the Imanis of the world—would continue the work gave her comfort.

DeFuniak Springs was not the same place it had been fifty years ago, but it hadn't shed its history entirely. The scars of the past remained etched in its streets and its buildings, but the future belonged to those willing to heal, willing to face the discomfort and the truth of what had been done. The lake, once a symbol of exclusion, now represented possibility—a place where the past and future could meet, where Black and white families could share the same space, swim in the same water, and imagine a future together.

"I believe in this town," Malaysia said quietly, breaking the silence. "I believe in you. And I believe that someday, you'll look back on this place and be proud of what it's become. The road's long, but we're on it. And we'll get there, together sweet as Tupelo Honey!" she said.

Imani smiled softly, the weight of her grandmother's words settling into her heart. "I hope so, Grandma. I really do."

Malaysia reached over, taking Imani's hand in hers, their fingers interlaced in a quiet symbol of solidarity, of generations bound together by the same fight, the same hope for a better future.

"Keep hoping," Malaysia whispered. "That's how real change happens."

And as the sun dipped lower, casting the lake in hues of gold and amber, Malaysia felt, for the first time in a long while, that perhaps, just perhaps, the new Southland she had dreamed of was beginning to take shape.

The lake shimmered under the fading light of the afternoon, its surface a calm mirror of golds and purples, broken only by the occasional ripple from a distant swimmer. Malaysia Jackson let her eyes rest on the water, feeling the weight of time press gently on her chest. She leaned back on the bench, allowing her memories to drift in the quiet stillness, the sound of children's laughter mingling with the soft rustle of the wind through the old oaks. So much had changed since the days of her youth, and yet, sometimes it felt as if nothing had.

At seventy-three, Malaysia had witnessed the long, uneven march of progress in DeFuniak Springs, a small town that had been shaped, and often misshaped, by its history. As a young girl, she never could have imagined sitting here by this lake—one that had been off-limits to her because of the color of her skin. She'd grown up in a town where her had been pushed to the edges, both figuratively and literally, always kept at arm's length by the invisible lines dividing Black and white.

Today, families of all colors picnicked on the shore, children chased one another through the park, and couples walked hand in hand, gazing at the tranquil water. The scene was peaceful, and on the surface, it looked like the kind of town people dreamed of raising their children in. But beneath that peace lay a history that could not easily be erased. There were wounds that still hadn't healed, scars left by years of oppression and division.

"Grandma?" Imani's voice called her back from her thoughts.

Malaysia turned, her face softening at the sight of her granddaughter. Imani had grown into a beautiful young woman, tall and graceful, with sharp eyes that saw through the world's façade. Sixteen now, she had her whole life ahead of her, and Malaysia often wondered what kind of world Imani would inherit. Would it be a better one than she'd known or would the struggles Malaysia had lived through continue to haunt the future?

Imani sat beside her, her curly hair tied back in a scarf, wearing that familiar look of contemplation Malaysia had come to recognize. "You ever think about how different things are now?" Imani asked, glancing out at the lake. "I mean, you always talk about how it used to be, and it's hard to imagine. Like, this place—it doesn't seem like it could've ever been so divided."

Malaysia smiled at the innocence of her granddaughter's words. Imani had been born into a new era, one where segregation was a memory and not a reality. But while the world had changed, Malaysia knew all too well that the past had a way of lingering in the present.

"Things have changed, baby," Malaysia said, her voice gentle but firm. "More than I ever thought they could. But that doesn't mean it's all behind us. Sometimes, the things that divide us—they're not so easy to see anymore. They don't look like they used to. But they're still there, under the surface."

Imani's eyes narrowed as she listened. "You mean, like how people act nice to your face but say things behind your back? I've seen it at school. Some of the white kids act cool with me, but I hear the stuff they say when they don't think I'm around."

Malaysia nodded. "That's part of it. You see, back in my day, people didn't have to hide it. If they didn't like you because of the color of your skin, they made sure you knew it. It was in the laws, in the way the town was laid out, in the way we lived our lives. We couldn't even sit by this lake, let alone swim in it. We had our own places, and they had theirs. And that's just how it was."

Imani shook her head, disbelief crossing her face. "That's so crazy. I can't imagine living like that."

"It was a different world," Malaysia said quietly. "But it's important you remember it. Because even though things look better now, we still carry the past with us. The town's changed, but some of the people haven't. They don't say it out loud like they used to, but it's still in the way they look at us, the way they talk when they think we're not listening. Racism doesn't just disappear because the laws change. It's deeper than that."

Imani leaned forward, her elbows resting on her knees as she stared at the water. "So, what do we do, Grandma? I mean, if people don't want to change, how do we move forward? How do we make things better?"

Malaysia sighed, a deep, thoughtful sound that carried the weight of her years. "We keep going.

We keep talking, keep pushing. We don't let them make us small. The future belongs to you and your friends, Imani. The work we started—it's your job to keep it going. You have to make sure this town doesn't fall back into the old ways, even if it feels like it's easier to let things be."

Imani sat quietly for a moment, processing her grandmother's words. "I don't want to live in a world where people hate each other because of something as stupid as skin color," she said finally. "I want The Springs to be better. For everyone."

"That's a good start," Malaysia said with a smile. "But you have to understand that healing takes time. It's not going to happen overnight. People hold on to their pain, to their anger. It's hard to let go of the past, even when you know you need to. But you—your generation—you've got a chance to build something different. You've got to keep talking, keep listening, and most importantly, keep showing people that we're all in this together."

Imani nodded slowly, but a shadow of doubt crossed her face. "But what if people don't want to change? What if we're always fighting the same battles and it goes on and on?"

Malaysia reached over and placed a hand on her granddaughter's arm, her voice full of quiet strength. "You don't fight alone, baby. You've got family, friends, a whole community behind you.

And remember—every little bit of progress matters. This lake? It's a small thing, but it's a symbol of what we can do when we don't give up. The fact that we can sit here together, that you can play here, swim here, without anyone telling you you're not allowed—that's a victory. It may not seem like much, but it means everything."

The sun was beginning to set now, casting a soft orange glow over the water, making it look like molten gold. Families were packing up their picnic blankets, calling out to children who were still running through the park, reluctant to end the day. Malaysia watched them, her heart swelling with hope and a touch of sadness. The scars of the past were still there... so were future possibilities.

Imani stood up, stretching her arms over her head. "I guess you're right, Grandma. Things have gotten better. But I'll do my part to make sure they keep getting better. For all of us."

Malaysia smiled, feeling a sense of pride rise in her chest. "I know you will, baby. And when I'm gone, I want you to remember that. You're part of something bigger than yourself. The work you do, the kindness you show, the fights you take on—they all matter."

Imani turned to her, her eyes filled with determination. "I won't ever forget, Grandma. I promise to always remember."

As they began to walk back toward the car, the last light of day fading behind them, Malaysia felt a deep sense of peace. The world was changing, slowly but surely. The new Southland was not a perfect place, but it was a place where people could come together, where the divisions of the past didn't have to define the future.

The lake—once a symbol of exclusion—was now a place where everyone belonged, a place where future generations could gather, learn from one another, and continue the work of healing the wounds that had run so deep for so long. Malaysia knew the fight wasn't over, but as she looked at her granddaughter, she felt hope rising in her chest. The future was bright, and it belonged to them all.

"We've come a long way," Malaysia whispered, more to herself than to Imani or anyone else. "And we've still got a long ways to go. But lord willin' we'll get there someday. Together!"

While the South grappled with unrest the northern cities were flaming in riots.

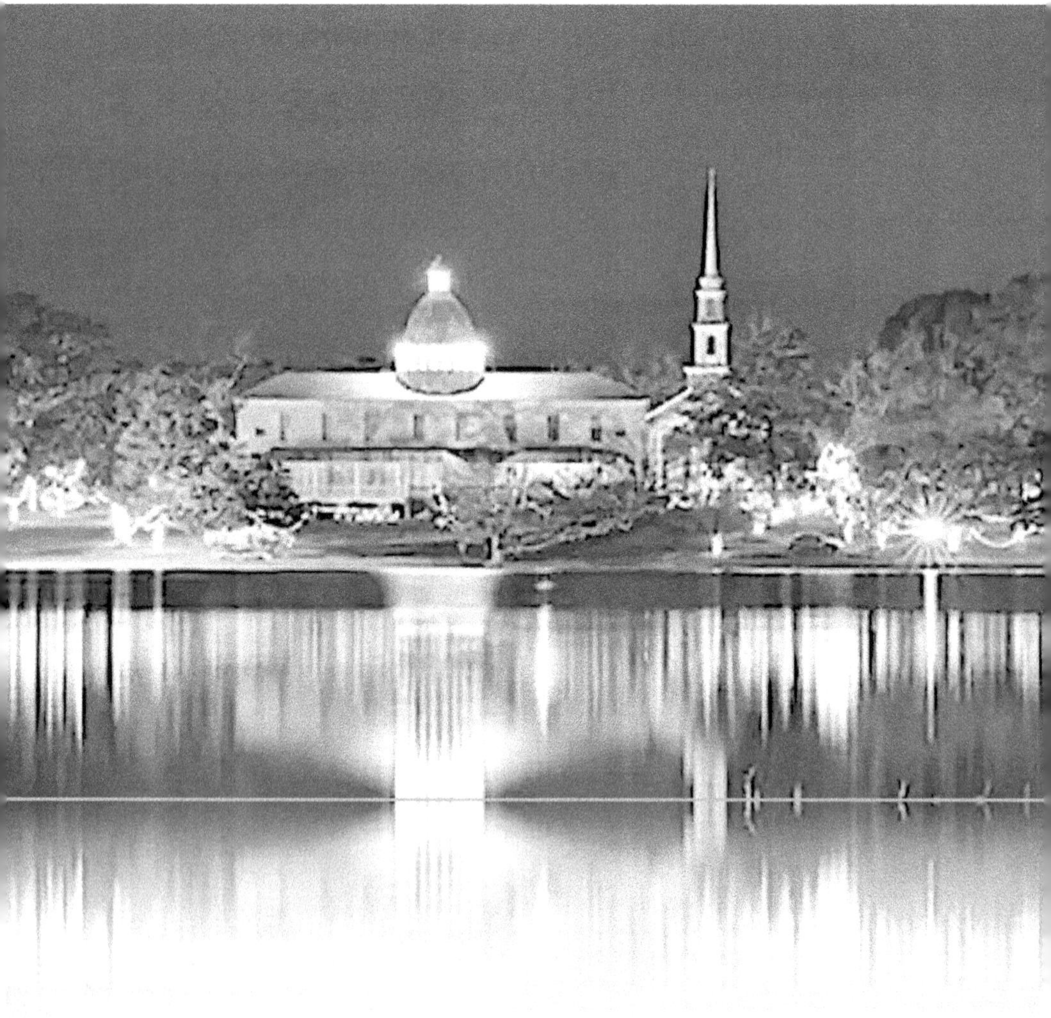

CHAPTER 10

Waters of Healing
Change Comes to The Springs Slowly

History has shown us that courage can be contagious and hope can take on a life of its own.
Michelle Obama

Denying racism is the new racism.
Bill Maher

The Future of Defuniak Springs was looking up. The sun dipped low in the sky over the small town, casting a golden hue over the Lake as Lynn Green leaned against the railing of the newly built boardwalk along the lake. It had been a long time since she had been able to enjoy this view without the weight of history pressing down on her shoulders. The lake, once a battleground of ideals and identities, had undergone a transformation—cleaned up, reopened, and now filled with families enjoying picnics and children splashing in the water. But beneath this surface of progress, Lynn felt the undercurrents of resentment and mistrust that still lingered.

The fight over the Confederate flag had stirred up old wounds that hadn't yet healed. The flag, once a common sight at local events and a symbol of pride for many in Walton County, had become a flashpoint for division. The community had grappled with its meaning, its legacy, and the very real pain it caused. Lynn could still recall the heated debates at town hall meetings, the faces of friends and neighbors split down the lines of ideology. Some insisted it was heritage, a part of their identity, while others saw it as a banner of hate and oppression.

As she watched the water ripple under the gentle breeze, she remembered the day the decision had been made to remove the flag from the town square. It had been a hard-fought victory for many, but even now, it felt bittersweet. The flag might have come down, but the attitudes that supported it had not disappeared overnight. Instead, they had morphed into something more insidious—an undercurrent of covert racism that was harder to pin down, harder to confront.

"Looks good, doesn't it?" a voice interrupted her thoughts. It was Gerald, an old friend from high school, who had spent years working as a local contractor. His calloused hands were shaded in the evening light, his hair slightly thinning but his smile still warm.

"It does," Lynn replied, forcing a smile. "But it feels like we're just painting over the cracks. If we have to force it in Federal court we will!"

Gerald nodded, his expression shifting to something more serious. "Yeah, I get that. People want to move on, but not everyone is ready to. There's still a lot of tension. Just the other day, I overheard some folks talking about how they wish things could go back to the way they were."

Lynn sighed, her shoulders slumping slightly. "It's frustrating. We're trying to build something better, and some people just can't let go of the past."

They stood in silence for a moment, watching the sun continue its descent, the shadows stretching long across the boardwalk. The laughter of children echoed in the distance, punctuated by the sound of a nearby grill sizzling. It was a scene of community, but beneath it all, Lynn could sense the underlying discord.

"Do you think it'll ever change?" Lynn asked, glancing sideways at Gerald. "I mean really change, not just this surface-level stuff?"

Gerald shrugged. "I think so. It's just gonna take time. The new businesses coming in, the younger folks moving back after college—they're more open-minded. But it's a slow burn. You know how stubborn the old-timers are."

Lynn chuckled dryly. "Stubborn is an understatement and he's too big for his britches."

"Still," he said, leaning against the railing with a contemplative look. "It's better than it was. People are starting to see that diversity can be an asset. The economy is improving. New restaurants, shops—there's a vibrancy to the place now that we haven't seen in years."

"True," Lynn conceded, glancing down the boardwalk at the new art installations that lined the path. The local artists had taken advantage of the revitalization efforts, and it felt like a new chapter was beginning, one that celebrated culture rather than erased it. "But every time I see someone raise the flag or make a joke that crosses the line, I'm reminded that there's still so much work to do."

"You're right," he said, the gravity of her words settling in the air between them. "It's like we're all walking on eggshells, trying not to trigger anyone. The thing is, the old ways of thinking are still in the back of people's minds. It's just more covert now, more subtle."

Lynn crossed her arms, leaning back against the railing, her eyes scanning the park beyond the lake. It was packed with families, but her heart felt heavy. The sounds of joy and laughter felt juxtaposed against the bitterness she knew still festered beneath the surface. "I hate that it's all so hidden. I want to know where people stand. It's easier to fight the outright racism than this quiet mistrust and subtle innuendo."

"Yeah," Gerald replied. "But we've got to keep pushing for change, even if it's hard. You've been a big part of that. Your work with the community programs, the push for inclusive events—people are listening, even if they're not saying it outright."

"I hope so," she said softly. "But it feels like we're just scratching the surface. And every time we take a step forward, there's a push back. I just wish people could see that we're all in this together."

"Maybe they will," Gerald said, his voice steady. "It's not going to happen overnight, but there are new generations coming up—kids who will grow up without the same biases, without the weight of the past on their shoulders. That's what gives me hope for the future."

As the last rays of sun dipped below the horizon, casting a warm glow over Defuniak Springs, Lynn felt a flicker of something akin to hope. It was fragile, tempered by the realities of the present, but it was there. They were making small strides, toward a future that would be better than the past.

"I just wish I could see it more clearly," she admitted, turning to Gerald with a hint of vulnerability. "I want to believe we can do this. I really do but sometimes I am not so sure. You can't make a silk purse out of a sow's ear!" she said.

"Then let's keep working at it," he replied, offering a reassuring smile. "Every small victory counts. And we're not alone in this."

With a newfound sense of purpose, Lynn felt the weight of her responsibility. She was part of a community, a thread in the fabric of a town slowly reshaping itself. And even as the old resentments simmered just beneath the surface, she could see the possibility of a brighter future—a Defuniak Springs that could rise above its past and embrace the change it so desperately needed.

"Together," she echoed, her heart steadied by the promise of progress.

Lynn took a deep breath, the scent of freshly cut grass mingling with the lake's dampness, a reminder of the summer still lingering in the air. The park was alive with activity: families setting up picnics, children chasing each other around the new playground, and couples strolling hand in hand along the water's edge. It was the kind of vibrant scene that made her heart swell with pride. Yet, the backdrop of recent history played on repeat in her mind—the protests, the town hall confrontations, and the echoes of anger that had filled the air just a few short years ago.

"I want to organize something," she said suddenly, turning back to Gerald with renewed determination. "An event that really brings the community together—something to celebrate our progress but also address what still needs to be done. And something to include the kids!"

Gerald raised an eyebrow, intrigued. "What do you have in mind? A concert?"

"Maybe a festival?" she suggested, her excitement building as she spoke. "A 'Unity Festival' or something. We could showcase local artists, musicians, food from different cultures—something that really highlights the diversity we're starting to embrace. We can invite everyone—Black, white, Hispanic. We need to show that we're stronger together."

He nodded slowly, his eyes thoughtful. "That could work. It'd be a good way to get people involved and open up conversations. But you know some folks might not be receptive. Not everyone wants to see change, especially the old guard."

"I know," Lynn replied, a frown creasing her brow. "But it's time to confront that head-on. We can't keep tiptoeing around the issues. The only way to heal these wounds is to bring them into the light. We need to create a space where people can talk, share their experiences, and understand each other. It's hard to hate someone when you know their story. We are more alike than we are different."

"True," Gerald said, his expression softening. "But you might get some pushback. There are still folks who will see this as a threat to their way of life."

Lynn straightened, her resolve hardening. "Let them come. I want them to see that we're not going away. We're not here to take anything from them; we're here to build something together. And if they can't see that, then maybe it's time for them to reevaluate their beliefs."

Gerald chuckled, the sound a mix of admiration and caution. "You've got fire, Lynn. Just be careful. You don't want to end up in a confrontation like we had last summer."

The memory flashed through her mind—the heat of that day, the shouts, the police sirens, and the violent energy that had rippled through the crowd. The tension had felt almost palpable, as if the air itself were charged with electricity. She had been scared, yes, but also invigorated, ready to stand up for what she believed was right.

"I can handle it," she assured him, a spark of determination lighting her eyes. "I'm not afraid of a little resistance. We've come too far to back down now."

As the sun dipped below the horizon, the sky turned into a canvas of purples and golds, and the park began to transition into evening. The laughter of children faded into soft chatter as families started to pack up their belongings, the light illuminating their faces as they shared stories and made plans for the next gathering.

"Okay, let's do it," Gerald said finally, breaking the momentary silence. "Let's plan this festival. But we need to involve everyone—local businesses, the schools, the churches. We can't have this be just a 'Black and white' thing. It has to be a community-wide effort."

"Absolutely," Lynn agreed, her heart racing at the prospect. "We'll set up a committee. We can reach out to the Chamber of Commerce and get their support. I'll start contacting artists and musicians, and we can have food trucks from different cultures. This is going to be our chance to show that Defuniak Springs is more than just its past."

"Let's do a brainstorming session this weekend," he suggested, rubbing his chin thoughtfully. "Get some people together, maybe at the café downtown. We can hash out ideas and figure out logistics."

"Sounds perfect," she said, a smile spreading across her face. "I'll make a list to invite!"

As they chatted about the details, Lynn felt a rush of excitement coursing through her veins. For the first time in a long while, she felt like they were moving forward, taking tangible steps toward a more inclusive future.

But even in her optimism, the shadows of doubt lingered in the corners of her mind. She knew that not everyone would welcome the changes she envisioned. In conversations around town, she'd heard the quiet grumbling about the "new direction" Defuniak Springs was taking—talk about "political correctness" and "overreaching agendas." Some still clung fiercely to the notion that their way of life was being threatened.

As they finalized their plans, a figure in the distance caught Lynn's eye. A group of young men stood near the park entrance, their laughter too loud, their body language too aggressive. She recognized a few of them from high school—kids who had been raised in the very heart of Walton County's tradition of resistance. They were looking her way, the grins on their faces unsettling.

"Lynn," Gerald said, noticing her distraction. "What's wrong?"

"Just some guys I used to know," she replied, her tone measured, though her pulse quickened. "I don't like the way they're looking over here."

"They're probably just looking to stir up trouble," Gerald said, his brow furrowing. "Something is Cattywampus, let's keep our distance."

But Lynn felt an odd pull toward them, a strange mix of curiosity and concern. What would they say if they knew she was organizing a Unity Festival? Would they dismiss it as another misguided attempt at change? Would they see her as a traitor to their community, someone who had turned her back on the values she was raised with? As the group drew nearer, she could hear snippets of their conversation—jokes laced with sarcasm, references to the old flag that had once flown so proudly in town. Their laughter hung in the air, and Lynn felt a knot tighten in her stomach. She took a breath, grounding herself and reminding herself why she was there and what was at stake.

"Whatever happens, I'm ready," she whispered under her breath, steeling herself for the confrontation that might come.

"Just ignore them," Gerald urged, noticing her tension. "We don't need to engage."

But as the young men approached, their confidence exuding from every step, Lynn couldn't help but feel that this was the very moment she had been preparing for—the moment to face the ghosts of her past head-on.

"Hey, Lynn!" one of them called, a cocky grin spreading across his face. "What's this I hear about a festival? Planning to bring a whole lot of trouble to our town? Hell will freeze over first!"

Lynn straightened, meeting his gaze with unwavering determination. "I'm planning to bring our community together, actually. Not everyone wants to live in the past."

His smile faltered for just a moment, surprise flickering across his face, but he quickly regained his composure. "Together? With them?" He gestured vaguely, as if referring to anyone who wasn't part of his circle. "I think you're going to have a hard time with that, sweetheart."

"Maybe," she replied, her voice steady, "but it's a fight worth having. It's time for Defuniak Springs to move forward. You can either be a part of that or stay stuck in the past. Your choice."

The group exchanged glances, uncertainty creeping into their bravado. "You think you can change anything?" another one challenged, his tone shifting from mockery to anger. "This town is ours. It always has been."

"Maybe you should consider that it belongs to everyone now," Lynn said, her heart pounding. "You don't get to decide who belongs here and who doesn't. That's the real change that's coming. Whether you like it or not."

With that, she turned back to Gerald, who stood with an approving nod, pride evident in his eyes. The tension in the air was thick, but Lynn felt a rush of exhilaration coursing through her veins. For the first time, she had confronted not just her past but the remnants of a mindset that had held her community back for far too long.

As she and Gerald walked away, the laughter of the group faded behind them, replaced by the sounds of the lake, the soft murmurs of families settling in for the evening. Lynn knew that the road ahead would not be easy; there would be challenges, resistance, and perhaps more encounters like this one. But with each step forward, she felt the promise of a brighter future solidifying beneath her feet.

"Are you ready for this?" Gerald asked as they reached the edge of the boardwalk.

"More than ever," Lynn replied, her resolve steeled by the confrontation. "It's time to show that change is not something to fear, but to embrace."

As they stood together, the setting sun casting a warm glow over Defuniak Springs, Lynn felt a sense of hope blossom within her. The fight was far from over, but she was ready to lead the charge, to face whatever came her way. Together, they would forge a new path, one that honored the past while embracing the possibilities of the future—a town that could rise above its history and become a community where everyone truly belonged.

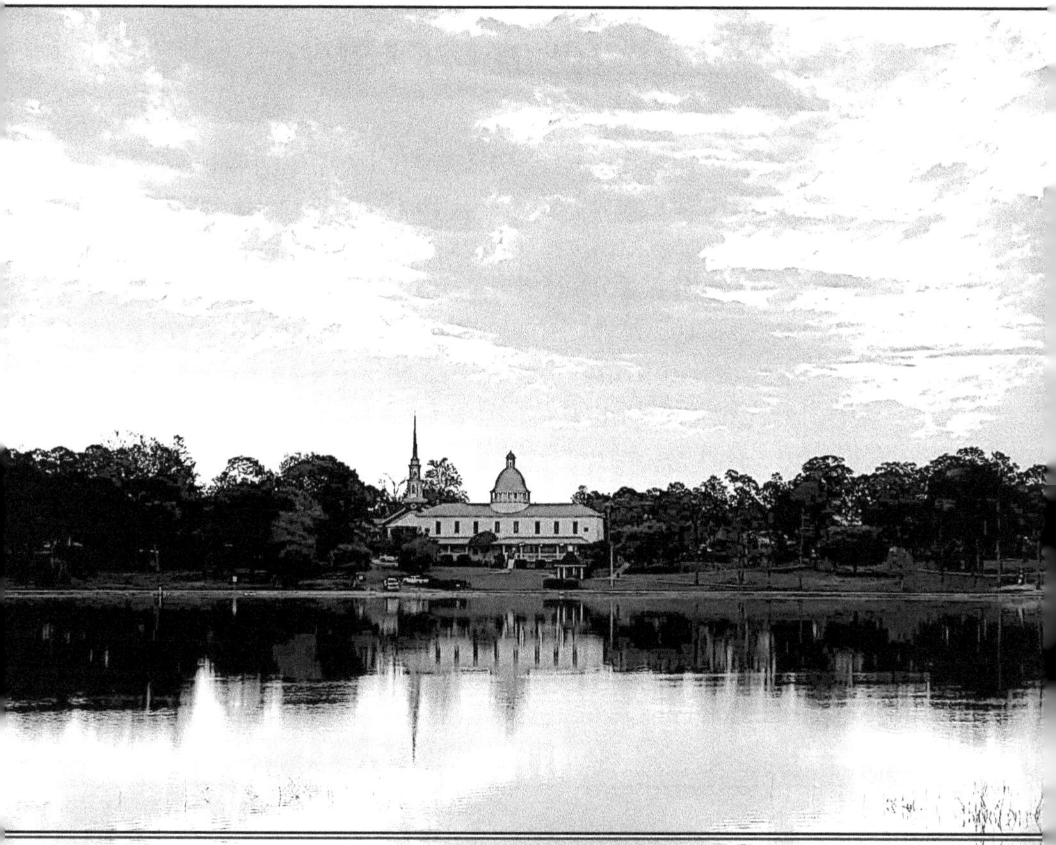

The Klan:
A Secret in the Open

The Ku Klux Klan in Northwest Florida had long operated in the shadows, its presence both feared and whispered about, especially in the smaller, rural towns that dotted the region. Invented a short distance away in Atmore, Ala., in Walton County and the surrounding areas, the Klan was never an official entity, yet its influence permeated local culture and politics. The organization's power ebbed and flowed with the tides of national racial tension, but in Northwest Florida, it found fertile ground to maintain its grip even until today.

The KKK first gained traction in Florida during the Reconstruction era after the Civil War. Many white

For years it was an open secret that the Klan held meetings secretly at night in the local Wallace Hardware store.

residents, feeling threatened by the newfound freedoms of Black citizens, saw the Klan as a means to preserve their social and economic power. In Northwest Florida, where agriculture and logging dominated the economy, the racial hierarchy was rigidly enforced, and the Klan became a vehicle for enforcing Jim Crow laws and resisting Reconstruction efforts.

For years, Klan members were able to operate with impunity. Lynchings were a terrifying and ever-present threat to Black residents, and though fewer were documented in Northwest Florida than in parts of Alabama or Mississippi, the specter of racial violence hung in the air. Local law enforcement often turned a blind eye to the Klan's activities, and some officers were even rumored to wear the hood and robe themselves.

By the 1920s, the Klan had experienced a resurgence nationally, and Northwest Florida was no exception. The resurgence was fueled by a toxic mix of racial animosity, economic uncertainty, and fears of modernization. The region, though geographically close to more liberal urban centers like Tallahassee or Pensacola, was culturally conservative. Many people here clung tightly to traditions rooted in segregation and white supremacy, making it fertile ground for Klan activity.

The Klan in Northwest Florida didn't just target Black citizens. Catholics, Jews, and labor organizers also found themselves on the receiving end of the Klan's wrath. The organization held public rallies, burned crosses, and terrorized anyone they deemed "un-American" or a threat to their vision of a white Protestant nation. Klan members in Walton, Okaloosa, and Holmes counties held secret meetings in barns, fields, and even church basements. By day, they were shop owners, sheriffs, or farmers; by night, they donned their hoods and robes, carrying out acts of intimidation and violence.

When the Civil Rights Movement gained momentum in the 1950s and '60s, the Klan in Northwest Florida saw it as a direct assault on their way of life. Desegregation orders from federal courts and civil rights activists pushing for equality enraged the Klan, and they responded with violence. Cross burnings increased in frequency, and there were several bombings and attacks on Black churches, homes, and businesses throughout the region. The fear of retaliation kept many Black residents in a state of constant vigilance.

Despite the violence, the movement for civil rights grew stronger. Local activists, supported by organizations like the NAACP, began to challenge segregation laws and practices in places like DeFuniak Springs, Crestview, and beyond. Demonstrations, sit-ins, and marches started to appear in these small towns, though they were often met with violent opposition. The Klan's influence, while still strong, was beginning to be challenged by federal intervention and the resilience of Black communities.

By the late 1960s, the national spotlight had shifted to civil rights struggles in larger cities, but Northwest Florida still simmered with racial tension. The Klan had been forced underground, but that didn't mean they were gone. The hoods might not have been as visible, but their members were still there—quietly ensuring that integration happened slowly and reluctantly, if at all.

Throughout the 1970s and even into the 1980s, the Klan's influence was felt in subtle but powerful ways. Black residents continued to face barriers to economic and social mobility. Businesses owned by Black families were often excluded from town resources, and political power remained firmly in the hands of white citizens who had ties—whether direct or indirect—to the old guard.
By the turn of the 21st century, the Klan's presence in Northwest Florida had diminished, but its legacy

remained. The scars of that era of terror and intimidation were visible in the persistent economic disparities, the segregation of neighborhoods, and the deep mistrust between Black and white communities. In some ways, the racism that once hid behind the hood now took on a subtler form—reflected in discriminatory housing policies, voter suppression tactics, and systemic inequities in education and healthcare.

Today, Northwest Florida has made strides toward becoming a more inclusive and diverse region, but the shadows of the Klan still linger in the memories of those who lived through it. Older residents can recall stories passed down about the nights when the Klan would ride through town, or about the people who disappeared, never to be seen again. Though the Klan's visible presence has largely disappeared, its historical role in shaping the racial dynamics of the region is undeniable. The fight for racial justice and equality in this corner of Florida continues, and for many, the past isn't just history—it's a constant reminder of how much more work remains to be done.

1856

DEFUNIAK SPRINGS
Jewel of NW Florida

For thousands of years, the area today known as DeFuniak Springs was inhabited by Native Americans. On March 4, 1881 the Florida State Legislature incorporated the Pensacola and Atlantic Railroad. As the survey party set out from Pensacola to survey the route for the railroad, they happened across an open area with a round lake. The party camped on the shores of the lake and their leader, W D. Chipley, declared this would the perfect spot for a town and ordered the virgin forest not be cut around this spot and a stop would be made along the line here. The location as named after Frederick DeFuniak, president of the Pensacola and Atlantic Railroad. First known as Lake DeFuniak the name was later changed to DeFuniak Springs.

Chipley, T. T. Wright, C. C. Banfill, W J. Van Kirk, and a few others worked to turn the small stop along the tracks into a town, forming the Lake DeFuniak Land Company in 1885. They began to sell real estate and find ways to attract people to the fledgling Heath and Hunting Resort they envisioned. Through a chance meeting while attending the Chautauqua Institution in New York in 1883, Van Kirk learned they were seeking a winter location to extend the program. After meeting with the leaders of Chautauqua and returning to DeFuniak Springs, the group decided this was the perfect draw to bring people to the new village.

In 1884, the Florida Chautauqua Association was formed and would operate in the town until 1936, holding its last annual Assembly in 1927. During this period a State Normal School, a free college to educate teachers, was created by the state, and operated from 1887-1905. McCormick University was established here but only operated from 1886-1888, when its buildings were destroyed by a hurricane. Palmer College formed in 1907 and operated until 1936. Along with the DeFuniak Business College, a preparatory school for the Normal School, as well as the Thomas Industrial Institute, the area was known as the educational center of the south during this period. The Florida Teachers Association was formed in 1886.

Arbor Day in the state of Florida started in DeFuniak Springs. The first planting of trees, in honor of Arbor Day in the state of Florida, were planted on the shores of Lake DeFuniak on

December 17, 1885 during the Southern Forestry Congress. It is believed some of those trees planted then still stand on the shores of Lake DeFuniak. After Chautauqua ended its run, DeFuniak continued to be a destination of choice for people seeking culture. An annual Music Festival in the 30s and 40s would draw thousands to watch bands, from all across the state.

The Walton DeFuniak Library, established in 1886 is said to be the oldest library in the state and is still operating as a library in its original building. Step inside and step back to an earlier time. Visitors can see current sections of the library as well as original editions that date back to the beginning of the library.

DeFuniak Springs once was also home to a Federal Agricultural Research station, as well as many orchards of blueberries, Le Conte pears, satsuma oranges, and other crops that were shipped to points all across the nation. DeFuniak Springs was also the location of two large sawmills that provided high quality yellow pine to the nation. DeFuniak Springs was also home to 22nd Governor of Florida, Sidney J. Catts, whose accomplishments include reforms in the treatment of the mentally ill and of convicts. He also began road improvements, tax reforms and labor reforms. He appointed a woman to his staff and endorsed suffrage for women. Statewide Prohibition Act was also passed at his prodding.

Many of the same things that made DeFuniak Springs so popular in its early years are still found here today. A quiet friendly community, today it still hosts cultural events like the Florida Chautauqua Assembly, Florida Chautauqua Theater, Grit and Grace, various Arts and Crafts groups, and a sense of community unique to itself. The historic district has changed very little over the years. Many of the homes built in early years, by visitors to the Florida Chautauqua who moved here from the north, along with business men of the time, still stand. Homes built by people like Wallace Bruce, internationally known author, lecturer, longest president of the Florida Chautauqua, and former U. S Consul to Edinburgh Scotland, as well as Isabella Alden known by her pen name Pansy, who wrote many loved Christian children's novels, to name a few.

Today the historic train depot, owned by the City of DeFuniak Springs, houses the Walton Heritage Museum. The City also owns the Chautauqua Hall of Brotherhood, which was built to replace the old Tabernacle auditorium built in 1884. Built in less than a year, the new Hall of Brotherhood was first used February 3rd, 1909 for the opening exercises of the Florida Chautauqua. At that time it was known as the most modern auditorium in the south with color dissolving lighting, seating for 4000, and a grand entryway designed to look like the US Capitol. The stage in the auditorium was said to be the largest in the south and able to hold 100 actors.

In 1975 hurricane Eloise destroyed the recently restored auditorium, so today only the front lobby and classroom portion remain and are rented out for special occasions such as weddings, birthdays, and reunions. Historic downtown remains much as it did when visitors would arrive by train 100 years ago; the buildings retain their historic look.

Courtesy City of Defuniak Springs
Public Affairs Dept.

Acknowledgments

The NW Florida Historical Society

Walton County PAO

City of DeFuniak Springs

The History Channel

U of West Fla. History Department

Walton Co. Heritage Association

Walton County Heritage Museum

WEAR TV3

The Walton County Sun

The Tivoli Historical Society

Northwest Florida Daily News

The Heritage Center of Freeport

WPLG TV10

Panhandle Historic Preservation Alliance

Walton Tribune

Read reviews on
goodreads

★★★★★
"Awesome! It was like I was there at the battle. A GREAT read."
-Reader Review

Now Available

- Book
- eBook

Coming Soon!
- Audiobook
  On Audible

- Kindle
- Apple
- BaM
- Barns & Noble
- Amazon
- Smashwords

www.authortommcauliffe.com

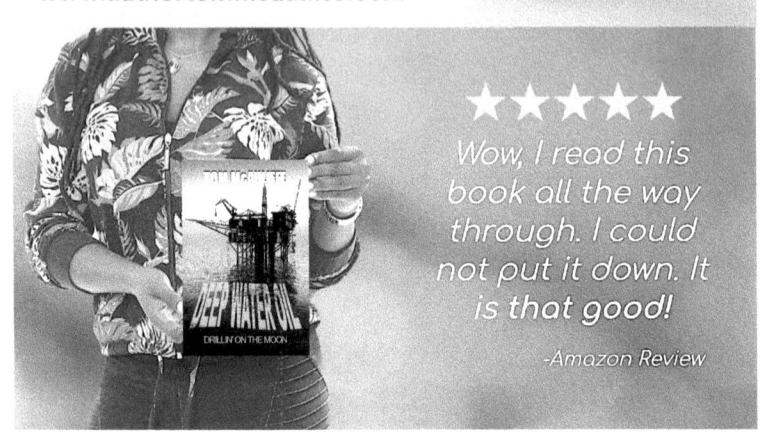

★★★★★
Wow, I read this book all the way through. I could not put it down. It is that good!
-Amazon Review

Please Visit:
www.authortommcauliffe.com

Please send questions to:
Bookinfo@nextstopparadise.com

Please Leave a Review!

Member:

Alliance of Independent Authors
Military Photojournalists Association
Emerald Coast Writers
Florida Writers Association
Alliance of Independent Authors

Books by Author Tom McAuliffe

- **Mr. Mulligan** - *The Life of Champion Armless Golfer Tommy McAuliffe*
- **Nuts!** - *The Life & Times of Gen. Tony McAuliffe*
- **Throttle Up** - *Astronaut Teacher Christa McAuliffe*
- **Mad Dog!** - *Detroit Tiger Dick McAuliffe*
- **Charmed** - *From Motown to Combat & Back*
- **Almost** - *The Road to the Grande*
- **Thunder Road** - *Goodyear, God & Gatorade*
- **Buddy, Brian and Me** - *A Spooky RnR Story*
- **Frozen** - *A WWII Mind Over Matter Tale*
- **Soft Shell** - *Teddy the Talking Turtle*
- **Max and Me** - *Paws Across the Water*
- **Off the Rock** - *Escaping Alcatraz*
- **Deepwater Oil** - *Drillin on the Moon*
- **Who Won?** *The 2024 Presidential Election*
- **No Place Like Home** - *The No BS Guide to Real Estate*

Books - eBooks - Audiobooks
On sale at Amazon, Kindle and your favorite local independent book store!

Also Available at:
WWW.AUTHORTOMMCAULIFFE.COM

MAX AND ME
A Story of Hope
Tom McAuliffe

OFF THE ROCK
Escaping Alcatraz
From the Award Winning Author of 'Mr. Mulligan'
Tom McAuliffe

Detroit Tiger Dick McAuliffe
MAD DOG
From the Award Winning Author of 'Mr. Mulligan'
Volume 4: The McAuliffe Series
TOM MCAULIFFE

Buddy Brian and Me
Star Bar
Tom McAuliffe

Soft Shell
Teddy the Talking Turtle
Tom McAuliffe

ALMOST
The Road to the Grande
Detroit Bands of the mid-to-Late 60's... You Almost Remember!
TOM MCAULIFFE

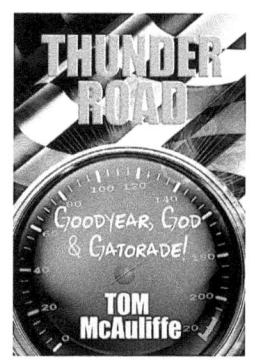

THUNDER ROAD
Goodyear, God & Gatorade!
TOM McAULIFFE

TEACHER ASTRONAUT CHRISTA MCAULIFFE
THROTTLE UP!
FROM THE AWARD WINNING AUTHOR OF 'MR. MULLIGAN'...
NUMBER 3 IN 'THE MCAULIFFE SERIES'
TOM MCAULIFFE

Mr. Mulligan
Sometimes Life is a Do Over!
The Life of Champion Armless Golfer Tommy McAuliffe
TRUE STORY
TOM McAULIFFE

FROZEN
A WWII Mind Over Matter Tale
Tom McAuliffe
From the Award Winning Author of 'Mr. Mulligan'

From the Award Winning Author of 'Mr. Mulligan'
No Place Like Home
The No BS Guide to Real Estate
•Buying •Selling •Investing
Realtor
TOM McAULIFFE

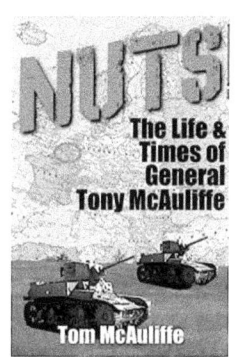

NUTS!
The Life & Times of General Tony McAuliffe
Tom McAuliffe

100% HUMAN
CREATED CONTENT

written by humans
not by AI

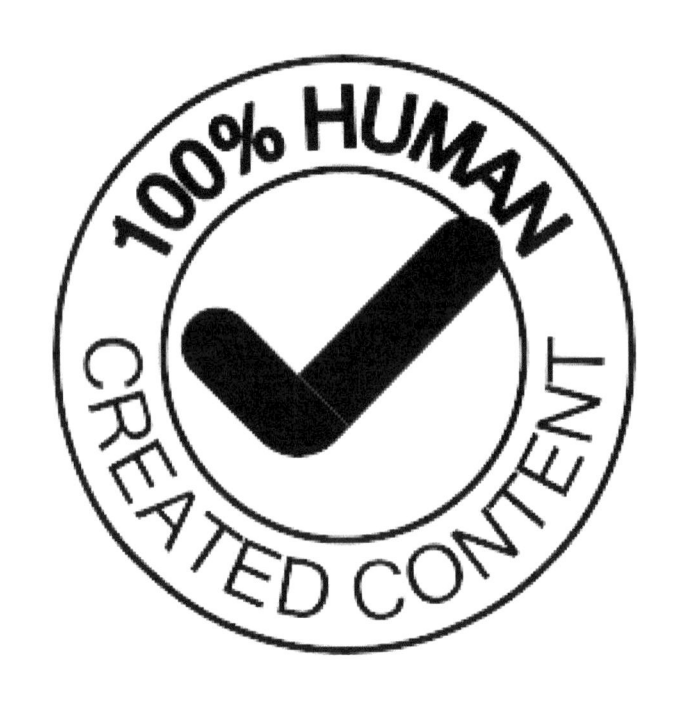

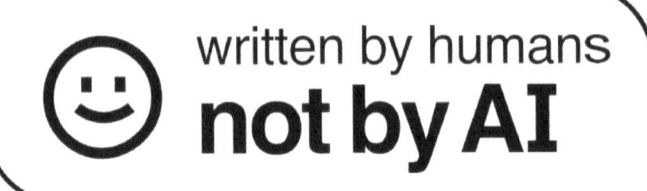

www.ingramcontent.com/pod-product-compliance
Ingram Content Group UK Ltd.
Pitfield, Milton Keynes, MK11 3LW, UK
UKHW022123211224
452733UK00012B/768